MOTHERNIGHT

Sarah Stovell

First Edition

Proudly published by

Snowbooks Ltd.

120 Pentonville Road

London

N1 9JN

Tel: 0207 837 6482

Fax: 0207 837 6348

email: info@snowbooks.com

www.snowbooks.com

British Library Cataloguing in Publication Data

A catalogue record for this book is available from the British Library.

ISBN 978-1905005-80-2

Printed in Great Britain

For my grandmother
Audrey Stovell.

For Gram,
With love

Prologue

My grandmother once said that it scared her, the way I loved things.

I was five or six years old then, and full of weakness for anything that seemed ugly and abandoned. I admired beauty, in passionless ways, but I never felt any need to keep or protect it because I knew I could rely on others to do that for me. Beauty was its own saviour. Its loss would always be mourned by someone.

But ugly things broke my heart – how they lived on forsaken by everybody, and so loathed. So to make it up to them, I sought them out and cared for them, and I loved them ferociously. Sometimes the things were people; others were just shabby toys.

But my grandmother said that it scared her, the way I loved things.

Part One

I

Along with a few of the things that held them together – a bank statement, a quote for repairing the ivy damage at the side of the house, advance notice of September's increase in school fees – the letter that was inevitably bound to pull them apart arrived in the morning's post.

It was Katherine who opened it. She sat and read it in the moments between pouring coffee and hosing down her youngest child's highchair, covered by then in cold porridge and warm milk – signs of her reckless independence now she was eighteen months and insisted on feeding herself.

She reached the end of the page, then passed it across the table to Gus without a word. Like much of their post, it had come addressed to Mr and Mrs Hartley, although strictly speaking, there was no Mrs Hartley anymore. She'd died twelve years ago, and Katherine – despite almost immediately moving into her house, having sex with her husband, and later giving birth to three children in her bed – hadn't conquered her name and become Mrs Hartley herself. Neither had she become the adopted mother of Mrs Hartley's only child, the seventeen-year-old girl Katherine never wanted to see again, but would unfortunately always have to.

She lifted Lily out of her seat and put her on the floor among wooden blocks and plastic pirates. Carrying the highchair onto the patio, she glanced over at Gus and failed entirely to read his expression. Wherever Leila was concerned, he stayed poker-faced and wordless.

Leila. Katherine turned on the tap outside the back door and aimed the hose at the highchair. Leila was his and he wanted her home. She moved a hand protectively over her middle and felt the hard swell of her fourth baby, due in the summer, and who she didn't want the girl to come anywhere near.

Today's letter was from Leila's housemistress. As she'd read it, there were parts that made Katherine want to laugh, but in the end, it was fear and unease that stayed with her. Already, she knew Gus was going to disregard it. He'd also disregard her fear. Leila would still be coming home.

She turned off the tap and wound the hosepipe back round its metal frame. The day was warm. She left the highchair to dry in the sun.

Back in the kitchen, Lily was crying. Grace, their five-year-old, had come downstairs from her room, dressed by herself in bright pink trousers and a green flowery jumper. Gus didn't look up as Katherine walked in. He was still reading. Perhaps, she thought, that was why he'd left Lily to cry.

She picked the child up and handed her a cup half-full of milk, left on the table from breakfast. She turned to Grace and asked mildly, 'Is that what you're planning to wear today? Remember we have to go out later.'

'Yep. Both of them are my favourites.'

Gus glanced up from the letter. 'That doesn't mean they go together.'

His voice was deep and unnecessarily gruff. Grace's bottom lip began to quiver. Katherine stepped in and smiled. 'It's all right. You look extraordinary.'

Grace, relieved, skipped off to the playroom. Lily squirmed out of Katherine's arms, abandoned her milk on the floor, and ran after her.

Katherine loaded the dishwasher in silence. Beneath the window, the last of the season's daffodils were out. She'd pick some later, and take them to Alfie. They weren't allowed to leave presents anymore, only flowers. The council had put a notice in the parish magazine. Presents made the churchyard untidy. There were no exceptions.

Eventually, she heard Gus drop the letter on the table. She turned round to face him.

He looked at her. 'What crap,' he said.

She shrugged. 'Ok.'

'I don't know why they have to treat this thing as though it's some dreadful scandal.'

'I don't know why, either, Gus. Perhaps there's more to it than they're willing to say in the letter.'

He pushed back his chair and stood up. 'It's a huge overreaction on their part.'

'Is it?'

'She hasn't done anything wrong.'

'No. Not really. She's nearly eighteen.'

Her words took away some of his force. He sat down again.

She could hear the shuffle of paper as he read through the letter, defended and in contempt. *Dear Mr and Mrs Hartley.* It surprised Katherine when she'd opened it, to find that after nearly eight years, they would still make such a fundamental mistake… *At this time of year, we often like to contact the parents of our sixth form girls to keep them informed of their daughter's progress during this crucial A Level period.*

I am delighted to say that, as usual, we have no concerns whatsoever about Leila's academic welfare. She is, once again, excelling in all her chosen subjects, and we are enormously proud of her recent acceptance at Queen's College, Oxford, where we are certain she will flourish and continue to achieve at her usual formidable standards.

We would, however, very much appreciate the chance to speak to you about our one concern for Leila. We are sorry to address this in a letter, but haven't been successful in our attempts to reach you by phone, and we do feel that, while the situation does not pose a risk to Leila's position in the school, it is nevertheless becoming a matter of some urgency.

Over recent months, Leila has developed an extremely devoted friendship with another young lady in the school, Olivia Rudham, who has been her roommate for the last four years. We certainly like to encourage closeness amongst our girls, particularly during the adolescent years, when many find a second family among their fellow boarders, but we are a little worried that this friendship might be progressing beyond those boundaries that we as a school and, indeed, society in general, deem acceptable for two young women.

Like Leila, Olivia is expected to perform very well in this summer's public examinations, and we would be very disappointed if either girl became distracted from her studies by an improper personal relationship.

I would appreciate it if you could telephone the school office and arrange a time, if you are willing, to come and speak to us confidentially and in further detail about this. We understand from the girls that there are plans for Olivia to come home and stay with Leila for the summer holidays before they move on to their respective universities, but we feel that perhaps it might be beneficial for the girls to have a period of separation, so that they can pursue their individual lives in a less claustrophobic fashion.

We look forward to seeing you again. With our very best wishes and our hopes for a speedy resolution of this rather delicate issue.

Janet Drew

Senior House Mistress

The Sixth Form Boarding House

Gus folded the letter and put it back in the envelope. Without raising his head to look at her, he said, 'I suppose there is no point in asking you to deal with this?'

Katherine hesitated, not because she was unsure of her answer – what answer could there be, except *No*? – but because she wanted, at all costs, to avoid an argument. There was still Lily to dress, shopping to be done, a walk with the girls to the churchyard, flowers for Alfie…

She said, 'I don't think so. Leila and I aren't close enough.'

'Right, then.' He stood up.

'Gus…'

He faced her. 'It's fine. I'll sort out a way of dealing with this. But I am still bringing her home for the summer.'

She turned away from him and held her hands over her belly again, caressing the baby boy beneath her skin. She felt him move, the flutter of one watery kick. She raised her eyes heavenward. *Please don't let them stay for long.*

II

Olivia

I found a new florist on the seafront, selling bunches of yellow roses and gold twigs full of berries. The berries were white. They seeped, and could have been poisonous, but they looked just right spread among the roses like that, tender and translucent as newly-hatched jellyfish.

I bought a bunch for Leila. As I slogged back up the hill to our school, I lowered my face into them and inhaled, and I thought I could smell her there, lingering among the berries, sad and sweet, but of course, that was just a romantic notion. When you loved someone and couldn't be with them, it was easy to imagine them there in anything that looked or smelled alluring.

Until about a month ago, she and I shared a room. It was official then, there for anyone to see on the list in the housemistresses' office: *Room Cordelia – Leila and Olivia*. I'd never understood why they gave the rooms those names. They were all characters from Shakespeare, and we had the most boring one of the lot. It was possible they'd thought virtuous

Cordelia would instill us with a sense of duty and make us behave, but there was no chance of that anymore, not now.

That was how we ended up moving. Because Cordelia's influence failed. They put me in Desdemona and Leila in Ophelia. I said to Leila that the housemistresses had it in for us – clearly, they wanted us destroyed by men – but she didn't believe they were aware of such subtleties, and it was simply that the school was bourgeois and pretentious. There was no reason, as far as we could see, why the rooms couldn't just have numbers. The literary labeling was an affectation and probably aimed more at the parents than the girls. It was supposed to reassure them, when they dropped us off on the first day having signed cheques for thousands of pounds, that if nothing else, we would all leave this school able to recite the name of every character in the Complete Works of Shakespeare – a crucial bluffing skill for the posh but not very bright (of which there were many; the school was non-selective; you only had to be rich).

Leila liked her new room. The one we'd shared before overlooked the primary school, and that had begun to send her crazy after a while and she hated it there. She used to go up to the office every week, telling the house staff she wanted an exchange, although she didn't mention the crazy side of things. She just said she wanted a view and some peace and quiet. The housemistresses fought against her for a month or so, but then all of a sudden, it was granted: new rooms for both of us, and single ones at that. Though that part didn't please us at all.

But still, we didn't take any notice now of the rules about staying in our own rooms and not leaving them after ten-thirty. Now we had two rooms between us, all ours, and we'd worked out ways of being together every night. Leila was willing to lock the housemistresses in the cleaning cupboard if she had to. She knew where the key was kept because of all the time she'd spent in detention, scrubbing out the toilets and chasing pubic hair round the showers, trying to get each curl down the plughole without using her hands. However bad she was, no one was ever going to expel Leila. She was far too clever. They needed her on the exam grade statistics

– the propaganda they sent to parents at the start of every year.

From the outside, Rotherfield Hall looked like a prison. There were even bars on some of the windows to stop the younger girls from falling out or, more likely I thought, to stop the older men from climbing in. They called the style of the building Gothic, and Leila once said its hostile appearance was why they'd sent her there –because Katherine had intended it as a punishment.

My room now was at the front. You could see it from the road as you approached. I carried on slogging. Like everything else at our school, the hill leading up to it wasn't to be taken lightly. Between that and the bars on the windows, we were well protected.

I walked through the main entrance and up the staircase to my room. It was smaller than Leila's, but not by much. Hers was at the other end of the building, and two flights up. They'd put us as far away from each other as possible, no doubt hoping laziness would get the better of us. Clearly, none of them had ever been in love, or if they had, it wasn't real love – not the sort where you would move heaven and earth and everything on it just to touch someone. Two flights of stairs and a corridor weren't going to stand in our way.

I arranged the flowers in a vase and stood it on the desk, next to my pile of Classics books. Mine were in translation. Leila's were in Greek. That was the main difference between Leila and everybody else – she could be bothered. Classics was the only lesson we were separated for. The others – English, History, and French – we took together.

Thinking of her made me sigh. I knew she'd be sad when she came back, which was why I'd bought her the flowers – because she was always cheered up by beautiful things. But there were times when I thought I'd have to take her a whole earth full of beauty, and not just eight stems of yellow roses, if I really wanted to make her happy again.

I opened the wardrobe in the corner. We hid bottles of wine in there among our clothes, but we had to be careful about it, because now they'd grown suspicious of us. They never used to be. The two of us had always been thought of as intelligent and hard-working, and if you were intelligent and hard-working, you could usually get away with a lot.

There was a bottle among the folds of Leila's black velvet coat, which she kept in my room because there was no space in hers. I poured it into the tumblers we'd taken off the stack in the refectory, and then I sat down and waited for her to come home. She was away in town, having lunch with her father. That was the way she spoke of him. She never said *Dad.* She always said *My father*, and I thought it sounded so possessive and yet so remote, as though he might have been one of those ravens at the Tower of London – the ones that had their wings clipped so they couldn't fly away, even though no one knew what they were for, or what good they did. They only knew they were important, and it would be a disaster if they ever let them go.

•

I was brought up by my grandmother, when I was very young. My parents tried nannies for a few years, but none of them ever stayed, so my father's mother moved in to take care of us. Our home back then was a five-storey town house in Jericho, Oxford. It was usually full of staff and empty of family and my grandmother disapproved of that, which was why she came to live with us. The staff all lived on the top floor because my mother didn't like them cluttering up her living space. They were usually foreign, which meant that my parents barely had to pay them anything because all they needed was a roof over their heads and a pittance they could send back to their families to make them feel like millionaires. That was the way my mother put it, anyway. She expected them to work flat-out and be grateful. Her image of herself was as a benevolent provider of opportunity.

Soon after my grandmother died – suddenly, at the age of sixty-one – my father's firm offered him a transfer to New York: huge amounts of money, with a luxury rental apartment thrown in. He took it, of course, and they moved there, and let out their house in Oxford, and then never came back. I was eight and my brother was ten, and we stayed in England and went to boarding schools in the countryside, instead of uprooting to a city full of dirt and noise, because in all my mother's dreams of maternity, she'd wanted her children to grow up amidst rural idyll, surrounded by trees and rivers and wildlife.

My father worked as a corporate lawyer, for one of the big companies. He said he didn't do it for the money, but I struggled to think of any other reason why someone would sell themselves – blood, flesh, heart and soul – to an office that bound him for hundreds of hours a week, and also at weekends. The strange thing to me was that he hardly had a chance to enjoy his wealth and so it put me off money, which struck me as being little compensation for the sacrifice of a family. The little I knew of him was miserable, and brutal with it.

As far as I could make out when I lived with them, my mother's role was simply to spend what he earned. She didn't work. She claimed she'd given it up to look after her children, but she never went back, even after the first nanny moved in, and she moved in pretty soon after my mother had given birth. Once I'd gone away to school, I only ever saw my parents at Christmas. The flights were too expensive, they said.

They planned for me to stay at my first school in Suffolk until I was eighteen, but a few years ago there was a scandal in the boarding houses attracting police and social workers, which made it into the national press. My parents found out about it on the internet, and took me away from there and brought me here, to Rotherfield Hall in Eastbourne, instead.

I was fifteen then, and it was when I met Leila. She was a year younger than me, and she'd been living here ever since she was nine, but skipped a year group because she was clever. That was what they did with the clever people – they rewarded them with an extra year of life.

We didn't always share a room. Because I started here mid-year, the lower school boarding house was already full, so they gave me a poky little bed off the sick bay corridor instead. It wasn't really a room. It was just an unused space without even a door, and I felt sure the nurses used to snoop through my things whenever they grew bored of sitting in their surgery day after day. They spent their lives in there, waiting patiently for nothing more serious than schoolgirls' menstrual casualties, which were usually just excuses to get out of playing hockey, or if they weren't, then there were girls in our school with gynaecological disorders so severe they shouldn't really have been alive.

Leila didn't have a roommate in those days. She was the only person in the lower school with a single room. She said it was because she used to scare people, because she had nightmares and often woke up crying. But after I'd been in the sick bay for so long, they decided to take the risk. It was the greatest kindness anyone ever did me in all my time here. Some of the others in the lower school slept six to a dorm with people they hated. In everything I'd read about boarding schools, the head teachers and governors always tried to make out that it was like being part of one huge family. It wasn't. Or if it was, then it was a dysfunctional family. Half the girls had eating disorders, and no one had any privacy, not even in the showers. The showers were all in one long block, separated just by a flimsy white curtain that always turned see-through as soon as the water hit it. Because of the poor ratio of showers to girls, they only let us use them every two days. It was written down on a list whose turn it was to consume the day's ration of hygiene. Vanity in the girls was strictly forbidden. We were told to take pride in our appearance, but never to the point of making ourselves attractive. Mainly, they believed in cultivating the inner person.

Once I'd changed rooms, the others all thought of Leila and me as lucky.

We had a sink we could wash our hair in if it wasn't our turn for the showers. But there were always down sides. In the summer, the room was boiling, especially at night. We weren't allowed to sleep with the windows open, so we threw off our covers and slept only in shorts. Then, around November, it grew freezing cold, and from there until the spring, Leila needed two duvets and she kept extra blankets at the foot of her bed just in case. I'd never felt the cold in the way that she did, and one morning, when we were lying awake in our beds waiting for the bell to ring and force us to breakfast, I said, 'Why are you always so cold, Leila? Are you ill?' And she said she didn't know why, she'd just always been like it, and it was why she hated to do PE outdoors.

Really, I think she was just lonely, and bereft around her heart. That was why no amount of heating or blankets could ever warm her, and it was why she always walked with her back hunched over and her arms folded across her chest. The staff used to shout at her for bad posture. They didn't know she was just trying to warm herself up inside.

•

I'd had friends at my previous school, but no one I was close to – not in the way that other girls were close. I felt distant from most of them, from the ones who shared makeup and secrets and nights top-to-toe in single beds. My world was quieter. I wasn't shy, but I was solitary, and after my days in classrooms with teachers and bells and reading aloud, I retreated. I learned how to shut the world out, coiling up into myself, sleek, like an animal.

When I met Leila, I could see that she shut out worlds, too. She was faultless at it. She did it all the time, and it was tangible – a deliberate aura that separated her from everyone else, as though she existed on her own, inside glass.

It was a Saturday when they introduced us, a grey morning in early spring, rolling in full of sea-damp and manure. Mrs Drew, our senior housemistress, appeared without warning in the doorway of my room on the sick bay corridor. She smiled at me. 'Olivia,' she said. 'I have news for you. A new room has become free. You'll be sharing just with Leila Hartley. If you pack up your things, I'll take you there now.'

I was surprised. For over a month I'd been here, living out of a trunk. I knew they were trying to arrange a better room for me, but no one had mentioned it for weeks, or given me any hint that they'd found something.

Clothes and books lay scattered around my floor. I threw them all back into the trunk, on top of everything I'd been too lazy to unpack and then re-pack. I could see Mrs Drew frowning at my slapdash approach.

Until then, I'd wanted a roommate, and a decent bedroom, but now I felt nervous about sharing with Leila. I knew who she was, although we'd never spoken. She was in my English class, and astonishingly clever. As far as I could tell, she didn't have any friends. She hardly even looked at people. Sometimes I'd seen her at lunchtimes, sitting on her own on the field, reading, scribbling down notes, losing herself, it seemed to me, in fiction.

Once I'd packed and was ready to go, Mrs Drew walked with me down the corridor and across the main hall to Leila's room. It had a small blue sign on the door that said *Jocasta* in bold letters. Unlike the sixth form block, the lower school rooms were all named after mythological characters from ancient Greece.

Mrs Drew knocked lightly on the door. There was no answer from inside. She edged it open, and I could see Leila there, sitting cross-legged on her bed, her hair hanging loose to her waist. She looked up.

'Leila, this is Olivia, your new roommate for this year. I'm sure you'll help her settle in.'

She stared at me, and so I smiled at her. She looked older than fourteen.

'Hello,' she said, and although her gaze was cool, there was warmth in her tone.

Mrs Drew smiled brightly. 'I'll leave you two girls to get to know each other. Your lunches are ready in the hall, whenever you're ready to pick them up.'

They always left us packed lunches at the weekends – white paper bags with hard cheese rolls and some crisps in them. There were never enough girls staying behind for the staff to open the refectory and serve hot meals.

Leila said, 'I've seen you here before on Saturdays.'

'My parents live in New York. I don't often go home.'

'I don't, either. My father visits a lot, though.'

I nodded.

She said, 'Do you go home in the holidays?'

'Not usually. I usually stay with guardians.'

'So do I.' She was silent for a moment, and then she said, 'I've never had a roommate before.'

'Really?'

'No.'

I looked around. Her half of the room was meticulously neat and organised. Books were arranged by size on shelves, the desk was lined with folders, and she kept a small pile of pretty, hardback notebooks on the table beside the bed. Those notebooks were the only personal things the room seemed to have. The walls, stark and white, stood bare. Other girls' rooms were full of photos – of their families, of holidays, of each other.

She noticed me staring and shrugged and said, 'Sorry. Brighten it up if you want to.'

'It's OK.'

I turned away, and felt sad. The room, like her, reeked of isolation.

•

She was clever, too clever. That was the thing, at first, which I thought kept her apart. Her mind was too old for her – it weighed her down. Our teachers didn't seem to know what to do with her, since they'd already moved her up a year. They put her in Enrichment classes and gave her more challenging books to read, but sometimes I thought they'd be better including her amongst the rest of us, instead of just pushing her further away.

As time passed, and I grew to know her, and admire her, and then to like her, I realised that it wasn't only her mind that separated her. It was grief.

I knew from the beginning that she never went home. I didn't ask her, but I could never understand why, because her house was only in the next county – just over the border into Kent, and barely fifty miles from here. Her father came to visit every Sunday. He took her out and bought her clothes and expensive food that she hid under her bed and shared with me in the evenings, when the meals in the refectory were too bad.

Once, when we were sitting on her bed, devouring strawberries and raspberries her father had picked for her, I said, 'Are you an only child, Leila?'

She wiped the juice away from her lips. 'I'm the only child of my father and my mother. My mother is dead. My father has had another child since then.'

Her voice was matter-of-fact and monotone. She hadn't looked at me when she'd spoken.

I said, 'Does he see the other child?'

She laughed shortly. 'Yes. She lives with him. She's about two now, I think, and I know they're planning another one.' She paused for a while, and then said, 'There was another child, too, a few years ago. A baby. Alfie. He died.'

'I'm sorry.'

She shrugged. 'It happens.'

'How old were you then?' I asked.

'Nine.' Her hand brushed against mine as she reached for another strawberry. She said, 'I came away soon afterwards. I haven't been home since.'

•

Another six months passed before she mentioned him again, and then told me the truth about why they'd sent her away. And even though we were in the sixth form now, and over four years had passed, she still barely mentioned him, although I knew she thought about it almost all the time.

Her father still came to visit her every Sunday, and she'd once gone back there for Christmas. She'd been sad and distant for weeks afterwards. Eventually, she told me she could never do it again. It was too awful, seeing Katherine there with the children.

This summer was supposed to be different, though, because we were leaving Rotherfield Hall, and the school wouldn't be able to arrange families for us to stay with in the way they usually did. Leila's father wanted her to go home, and she wanted me to go with her. I wasn't sure at first, because her family seemed like such a horrible place to be, but in the end I agreed. The alternative was that I stayed with my own parents in New York, and then I wouldn't see her for over four months.

A car pulled into the school driveway below my room. I glanced up and saw her father's 4x4, and watched as they came out and said goodbye. He embraced her for a long time, tightly, and then kissed her cheek before he climbed back into the car and disappeared down the hill.

I hammered on the window. She looked up and waved. Her hair hung around her shoulders, blonde and fine. There'd be the distant smell of the sea in it, and the taste of salt on her lips. She disappeared out of sight as she headed to the main door of the house. My excitement rose at the idea of seeing her again. I could never wait to see her, even when we'd only been parted for a couple of hours, or for a lesson.

I heard the staccato clip of her heels in the corridor outside, then the door opened, and she came in.

•

It was Saturday evening. Most of the others had gone home. Together, we dragged my desk over the floor to the window, so we could drink our wine looking out over the sea. That way, we could imagine ourselves to be on a Mediterranean balcony in summer, with all the freedom in the world, instead of stuck in an ancient school building, pretending there was nothing between us but sweet teenage friendship, and being threatened with toilet-cleaning duty if we didn't.

I sat on the table and she perched on the windowsill beside me and lit a cigarette, breathing the smoke out through the gap and into the air outside. The sound of children playing in the distance reached us. She always told everyone she'd wanted to change rooms for the peace, because where we were before was too close to the primary school, but we both knew it had nothing to do with all the noise. It was because of Alfie, and all her thoughts about how old he'd be by now, and the things he'd be saying and doing if he were still alive.

She lowered her hand to my thigh, and moved it lightly over my jeans. She stubbed out her cigarette on the bricks below the window, then brought it inside and wrapped it in tissue before throwing it in the bin. She said, 'My father's just seen fit to tell me that Katherine's pregnant again. It's due in August.'

Her tone was casual, but the words weren't. I knew without asking that it meant our plans for the summer would be cancelled.

III

Leila

The Japanese always burned their dead. After that, the bones were taken out of the furnace and the whole family piled round and picked them up with chopsticks. They put the bone of their choice into a jar, took it home with them and buried it.

It seemed a sinister ritual to me. It was the chopsticks that did it. I imagined myself gathering up my mother's or baby half-brother's bones with a knife and fork. The idea made me want to vomit, but I knew Katherine would have relished all the latent symbolism in the image. Ammunition. An illustration of my morbid fascination with death and the dead.

My mother died at thirty-five. My baby half-brother died at thirty-seven days. I didn't die, but I wanted to, for years. So did Katherine, once her child had gone. But then she had two more, and they kept her going, although needless to say, they never took Alfie's place. No one could do that. That loss was forever.

My family was the stuff of tragedy. Or it would have been, if the lack of noble emotion hadn't reduced us to the level of soap opera. Or folk tale, at best. We were changeling children, my friend Rosie and me: substandard replacements for the ones that got away, or never came.

If you could have a changeling child, then couldn't you also have a changeling mother? That's what I had. They'd cast mine away and replaced her with Katherine. Katherine and the child who died. Perhaps I killed him. Perhaps not. In either case, I was nine years old. Rosie was eleven, and culpable.

•

They had me at dawn on the Winter Solstice. 7.30am. I'd always been a trick of the light. My name was Arabic. It meant Dark as the Night. That was my father's favourite story about me, how I'd been dark at birth, but then I changed, until finally, aged three, there I was: blonde and pale, outshining the shadows of my name.

In Norse mythology, they called the solstice Mothernight. I always found that ironic.

•

'Have you had any dreams, Leila?'

The voice belonged to the woman. She was trying a direct approach. At that age, I didn't respond to the subtlety of symbols. Before they sent me away, before the baby was born, before anything really, she used to come to the school and talk to me. Her name was Mary, or Marie, or Maria. Biblical overtones. Maternal. Perhaps they were offering me subconscious comfort for my grief.

I met with her weekly in the room that only I knew about. It looked like another cupboard from outside, but when you opened the door there was a room full of dolls. They had missing arms or legs, or even, in extreme circumstances, heads. I used to think they were just old, but it would all have been deliberate. They were meant to get me talking, those plastic victims of infant crimes.

My mother had been coming to me in nightmares. Every night, she'd look down at me, smile, and hold out her hand. Her fingers glistened with rings, or knives. I was never sure which. *Come.*

She wanted me with her. That was what I knew.

But I didn't say that to the woman. Her injured dolls failed to move me. She didn't know I was bound to my mother by strictest loyalty, and loyalty meant silence.

I told Rosie about her eventually. But she was the only one.

•

My life got better once Rosie moved next door. My father and I lived in Ash Farm, the big house at the edge of the village. He worked long hours and wasn't often there. (An antidote to his grief.) He paid a woman with grey hair and a grey dress to come over and give me my tea. She smelled damp, and hardly spoke.

The old people next door moved out when Rosie moved in. My father had met Katherine by then. She brought me presents. Her most recent offering had been a set of finger puppets: two children, a woodcutter, his wife and a witch. I didn't mind Katherine at first, but Rosie put me on the right path about step-mothers straight away. I'd only read the fairytales. She'd seen the real thing. Rosie was adopted at seven. She'd spent most of her life with the wrong people.

'Who do you think he likes best?' she asked. 'You or her?'

'Probably her,' I said. I understood, even then, that nobody likes a show off.

She put her arm around my shoulders. 'I think so, too. It's obvious.' She picked up the finger puppet witch and examined it carefully. 'You know, she only buys you these presents because she has to. She has to pretend to like you so your dad will marry her. After a while, she'll turn on you. They always do. They only want the man. They never want the child.'

I nodded, and took it in. Alone in my room, I imagined it could be true. I'd found out for myself that Katherine was a cheat. She baked vanilla fairy cakes in the Aga, but she smelled of cigarettes.

She didn't know my gift. I could spot the real mothers, the tender ones, whose skirts were long. They smiled when they met you at the school gate. They hid boiled sweets in their apron pockets. They took your hand. They smelled of flowers and fabric softener. They did you no harm.

I knew, because I looked for them, and I remembered.

•

I liked visiting other mothers, but I never saw my own in daylight. It was summer the first time we went to find her. Rosie's idea. I was in the garden in the evening, sitting on a chair I'd taken out to the front gate, on the lookout for strangers. I never told anyone that. I was secretive. I kept a notebook. In it I wrote down the number plates of the cars that went past my house. If a stranger was driving, I wrote a description of him. I had plans to take my list to the police in case the strangers turned out to be the wrong type – the type who did you damage. Mine was a strong moral fibre. I wanted them sought out, punished before they came near me.

Katherine would have said this showed my early obsession with criminal behaviour. But Katherine knew nothing. Most games started out innocent. Lots stayed that way.

Rosie had lived next door for two weeks by then. I didn't know her, but we were bound to come together. We were the only children for half a mile. I wasn't allowed outside the garden and that, too, was because of the strangers. They told us about them at school. The staff were vigilant about it, every year.

They never said a word about the ones who weren't strangers. They never said a word about the people you knew. The ones in your house. Rosie knew, though. Rosie understood statistics.

I looked up and saw her wheeling her bike down the lane between our houses. Her hair was long. She wore it in one plait down her back. She stopped, and leaned over the gate. 'Do you want to go on a bike ride?'

I hid my notebook in the pocket of my sundress. 'I'll have to ask.'

'No, you don't. Just come.'

I hadn't known until then that disobedience was an option. I smiled, and went round to the barn where my bike was kept. My father wanted to turn the barn into an office, but no one would let him. It was listed, protected by people who knew better than him. Inside, the barn was full of dirt and old straw. I thought we used to have chickens, but I wasn't sure. My memory of the world before my mother died was bleary.

My bike was propped against the wall, dusty and covered in cobwebs. I hauled it out through the rickety door. An old doll of mine lay stuffed inside the basket on the handlebars, her dress covered in faded blue flowers. She was muddy and damp, but then, I'd never been a maternal child. I had no interest in dolls, or babies, or things that needed looking after.

I brushed some of the dust off the frame, and wheeled the bike out onto the lane. Rosie zoomed ahead. I had to pedal quickly to keep up. The wind in my eyes made them water. I sniffed.

Rosie looked back over her shoulder. 'Why are you crying?'

'I'm not. I never cry.' That was true. I never shed a tear. I astounded people with my fortitude.

She slowed down. 'They told me your mum died.'

'What?'

'They told me your mum died.'

No one ever mentioned my mother, even though they knew. They talked about her. They talked about her when I wasn't there. They made up lies. Just like I did.

Rosie's brakes squeaked as she clattered down the hill towards the church on the corner. She abandoned her bike in the grass outside the churchyard.

'What did she die of?'

I shrugged. 'I'm not all that sure. No one ever told me.'

'Do you miss her?'

'I don't know.'

Rosie lowered her voice to the ground. 'I thought they were divorced. I didn't know she'd died.'

I stayed silent as I wheeled my bike over the grass and leant it against the fence. Rosie followed me.

'Where's she buried?'

I looked up at the church and shrugged. 'I don't know exactly. Not here. There's a place like a garden. That's where she is.'

'Let's go and find it.

'I can't.'

'Of course you can. If you look.'

'I haven't got flowers. You need flowers to see graves.'

Rosie laughed. 'You don't. You don't need anything. You just need to know a dead person.'

We walked down a slope with a brick path that led to the furthest corner of the churchyard. A dried-up stream curled through the undergrowth. The graves at the back were black and ancient. On the ground among the trees lay shavings of damp bark, rusty drinks cans, cigarette ends.

Rosie snapped a twig from an overhanging branch. 'Look.' She dangled it in front of my face. A limp balloon hung off the end, like an old piece of white rag.

I put my hand out to touch it, but Rosie snatched it away and hurled it into the grass. 'You can't touch that. It's a rubber johnny.'

I could tell from the way she spoke that it was something forbidden and shameful. I thought about the bodies of the dead people, rotting away under the earth where I walked.

Half-way down, the path turned into mud. Brambles hooked our clothes, and shook raindrops over our legs. Rosie tiptoed over the furrows in the ground. 'This can't be right.'

'It is right. They don't put dead people in the churchyard anymore. It's too full.'

Rosie looked doubtful.

I saw the tops of gravestones through the gaps in the trees ahead of me, and stopped walking. 'Here. It's in here.'

The track opened out onto a long garden. The grass was leafy and thick, and scattered with slabs of marble and granite. It backed onto cornfields. Beyond them stretched the horizon, made purple by the hills.

We jumped over a ditch, and fought through brambles to get in. As always, there had to be obstacles to joining the dead.

Rosie peered down a row of headstones. 'Which one is hers?'

I faltered. There were more graves than I could remember. The only time I'd been there was the day they buried her. They'd put her in the grave, and made me throw a white rose in on top of her. The petals were covered with raindrops that showered the back of my hand. I'd licked them off. I thought they were going to taste of lemon sparkles, but they were just water. Plain water. At five, I was disillusioned. They told me she was an angel, but I knew she wasn't. I knew they wouldn't drop an angel in the dirt.

I said, 'I don't know which is hers. I think it's near a tree.'

'What was her name?'

'Elizabeth. But sometimes it was Liz.'

We hunted for her among the headstones. An old man in a tweed jacket stood by a grave and frowned at me as I walked past him. I was too young, in his mind, to know about death. I shouldn't have been there. Damp rose petals bruised under my feet and stuck to the edges of my sandals. I walked slowly. I wanted to tell Rosie to go away, or to say I didn't want to look anymore, but that would have started a row, so I said nothing.

'It's here! I've found it!'

I turned around. Rosie was standing triumphantly beside a marble grave that stood alone an upright beneath the papery trunk of a silver birch.

I raced over and Rosie pointed. 'Look, this must be it. It's got your name on it, too.'

In Loving Memory of
Elizabeth Hartley
Beloved wife of Gus
and cherished mother of Leila

At the foot of the grave, some flowers that had grown old and wilted and died were slumped inside a stone pot. Rosie fingered the white card tied around one of the stems. The ink was watery and faded.

'It's from your dad,' she said.

I looked. *Happy birthday, Liz. Still missing you. G.*

I snapped it away from the stem and slipped it inside the notebook in my pocket.

'What are you going to do with that?'

I shrugged. 'I don't know. Keep it.'

'You could give it to Katherine.'

I shook my head.

'Is she definitely your dad's girlfriend now?'

'Yes.'

'Do you like her?'

'She's OK.' I knelt down on the grass and picked daisies for the grave. There were no other flowers around.

Rosie sat beside me. 'Do you think she's nicer than your mum?'

'No.'

'Well, why's your dad with her, then?'

'I don't know. He must like her.'

'Does she know about your mum?'

'She might. My dad doesn't really talk about her.'

'Why not? She's his wife. His real wife, I mean.'

'My grandma says it makes him too sad.'

'Not very sad. Not if he's with Katherine now.'

We were silent for a while. I put the daisies on the grave.

'Do you think he'd have gone off with Katherine if your mum was still alive?'

I snapped. 'How should I know?'

Rosie stepped backwards and smirked. 'He probably would have done. She'd have made him, and then your mum would have died anyway. People die of broken hearts.'

I started walking away from her, back to the church and home. It was impossible to tell whether this was just a game.

•

Katherine's car was parked in the drive when I got there. I hadn't known she was going to stay again. I propped my bike against the fence and took the doll out of the basket, then crunched over the gravel and ducked under the willow tree to the garden path. The back door flew open. Katherine appeared. She was red-faced and cross.

'Where have you been, Leila? Your father is out looking for you.'

'I went on a bike ride with Rosie.'

She carried on telling me off, but I tuned her out. A trick I'd learned already.

I knew how to make myself invisible. I looked at the ground, and kicked at the gravel. I had no reason to listen. I pushed past her, and ran upstairs to my room.

•

My bedroom used to be an attic. When people came to the house, they didn't know it was there. It was hidden behind a wooden door on the landing, which opened up to reveal a flight of stairs leading to an archway at the top. Beyond the archway was my room. There was one window in the ceiling, and through it I could see blackbirds and crows and the outlines of chimney pots sticking out from the roof. When it was dark outside, the chimney pots would get bigger and then they looked like men trying to get in.

I laid the doll down in my bed. On my desk, I kept a secret chest. My grandmother had bought it for me on my eighth birthday. It had a tiny padlock and a key that I hid so no one could open it. All around my room were hiding places. Today, I emptied it out from the toe of one of my socks. I always swapped hiding places, just to be sure.

Inside the chest was a pot I kept my money in. At the bottom, under a packet of tissues and some miniature storybooks, was a photo of me with my mother. My father took it when I was a baby. He'd given it to me last week, when he was clearing out boxes from his room and taking them down to the cellar. I'd never seen a photo of her before. He used to say he didn't have any. Liar. Liar.

I picked up the photo and looked at it. On the back, in handwriting I'd never seen before, it said *Leila, aged 17 days.* My mother wasn't looking at the camera.

She was looking at me. There was love in those eyes, I was sure. I touched my mother's hair with my fingertip. It was blonde, like mine. There were times when I imagined that rubbing the photo three times at midnight would bring it to life. I wanted her out of my dreams. I wanted her here.

The front door slammed, and I jumped. It was my father coming home. I crept to the bottom of my stairs and listened to the voices drifting up from the floor below.

'She came back ten minutes ago. She's in her room. I told her off.'

'I'll speak to her in a minute.'

'She was very rude.'

Their words dropped. They became low and secretive. I imagined myself running down to the kitchen and presenting Katherine with the card from my mother's grave. See? You're nothing. He loved her, not you.

I put the photograph in my pocket with the card, then went downstairs to speak to my father.

•

Later, when I was in bed, Katherine came up to my room. She offered to read to me. I shrugged. I didn't care. I could read to myself. I could read beyond my years. Years beyond my years.

She read. When she'd finished, she put the book back on the shelf, and she saw the finger puppets. I'd made them a theatre. They were lying dead in it.

'Oh dear, Leila,' she said. 'What happened to your puppets?'

I turned over in bed and faced the wall. 'Someone killed them.'

Katherine was silent.

'I don't know who it was.'

'Well...Perhaps I can take them away, and see if I can mend them.'

I sat up. 'You can't. I already tried. They're dead.'

Katherine picked up the puppets and each tiny wooden head that had been cut off. Her voice when she spoke sounded sad. 'I'll have a go, anyway.'

And then away she went downstairs.

IV

Olivia

I liked Leila. Sharing a room made it easy to get to know her, and I found she wasn't the hard, aloof person she'd seemed to me before. She was funny and gentle. *And fragile*, I thought, as though the wit and reserve might fall away at any moment and leave her broken and exposed. But I always knew that she was in control. Everything about her was controlled. It was why she worked so hard. Her mind was the only thing she owned and valued, and she was never prepared to lose it.

Everyone admired Leila, even the teachers, and even when she was in trouble. There was boldness and innovation to the way she flouted rules, and her rebellion usually had its roots in the intellectual, which made it hard for them to punish her, or even tell her off.

Some girls at Rotherfield ran away to go to concerts, or to spend nights with boys from the grammar school up the road. But when Leila ran away, she went to London on her own for poetry readings, or to the theatre. They caught her once, about a month after I'd moved into her room. A strike on the underground meant she missed her train home and found herself stuck at Victoria. She phoned me; I said I'd lie for her. So at eleven, when the housemistresses came round on their nightly patrol, I told them she was sick. They didn't believe me. They kept coming back, every thirty minutes until the early hours of the morning.

'Where is Leila, Olivia?'

'I don't know.'

They asked again.

I told them again.

Eventually, just when they were ready to call the police, she walked in, rain-soaked and freezing. She'd taken a late-night bus, which broke down half-way to Eastbourne. She told me later that she'd got stuck talking to an old man with calloused hands and slurred words, and slippers on his feet in a thunderstorm.

'Where have you been, Leila?'

'I have been to London, Miss.'

'London! You are fourteen years old, Leila Hartley. Do you have any idea what London is?'

'Yes,' she said earnestly, but I could see she was laughing inside. 'It's a city of debauchery. But I didn't go there for that.'

'Well what, may I ask, did you go there for?'

'I went to see *King Lear*, Miss.'

'You went all that way to see *King Lear*?' Mrs Drew's eyes stood wide in disbelief and also, I thought, uncertainty. 'Do you think,' she continued, 'that King Lear would go all that way to meet you?'

Leila stared at her blankly. 'I wouldn't have thought so, Miss. He's fictional.'

From where I sat in the corner, I began to laugh. Leila's boldness shocked and impressed me. It was one of the first things I'd noticed about her – her refusal to be talked down to. Her wit made her anyone's equal.

Mrs Drew, looking slightly humiliated, gave orders for the morning: Leila was to be up half an hour early, so she could be escorted to the main school and presented to the headmistress for punishment.

She left the room.

Leila turned to me. 'She speaks like the editor of a Victorian porn magazine.'

I laughed again, but saw that she was still shivering in wet clothes. I took my towel off the radiator and passed it to her. She buried her face in it, and then her hair.

I turned away as she began to undress. Without meaning to, I knew every movement she made behind me. I learned the minute sounds of cotton as it shifted over her skin, and I learned the smell of her: cold and rich, like earth.

I said, 'Are you warmer now?'

'No,' she said, 'but I'll be all right.'

I continued facing away, but her reflection appeared in the mirror on the wardrobe door – her back, her waist, the shape of her, like moulded sand.

She stepped into her nightdress, then unhooked her dressing gown from where it hung beside her bed and wrapped herself in it. Years fell away from her. Instead of looking eighteen as she often did, she looked childish and vulnerable. I had the unexpected urge to embrace her.

Instead, I said, 'Are you worried about seeing the head in the morning?'

She shrugged, 'No.'

She lowered herself on to the edge of the bed and cupped her hands around one foot to warm it. Her hair, loose and wet, fell down past her face. She shivered again.

I went over to the sink in the corner of the room and filled a bowl with warm water which I carried back to her.

'Here,' I said, placing it on the floor. Then I took her ankles and lowered them gently into the water.

She looked at me and smiled. 'Thank you,' she said.

•

After a while, we began to spend all our time together. We were the only two girls in the school who never went home, not even for holidays. We found out later that it was why they'd put us together – in the hope that we would dilute each other's loneliness. We did.

During the times we weren't together – odd lessons where we were separately taught, afternoons when she had extra classes – I found myself thinking of her, and missing her, and looking forward to her.

We spent our evenings shut up in our room, away from the other girls, who we didn't like because they were noisy and giggly and spoiled and stupid. We talked. We talked a lot. We talked about everything we thought of. For the first time, there became no barrier for me between the things that went on in my mind and the things I spoke out loud. I knew she kept everything I said, and cherished it, holding my words like pearls.

Sometimes in the mornings, when it wasn't our turn for the showers, we'd wash each other's hair at the sink in our room. Her hair was long and soft, and when I'd first met her, I was envious. But now, when she leaned back over the sink and I ran water luxuriantly through it, and she closed her eyes, I wasn't envious anymore. It was a different feeling, something odd, without a name, but strong. It made me move my hand out of her hair and down over her face, across her skin, until finally she reached upwards and then brought my fingers across to her lips.

•

Neither of us had been with boys, not properly, not in that way. She was too shut off, and I had no interest. They were strange things to me – small, spotty, awkward around girls. Because she was so pretty, Leila had the capacity to render them speechless. It was a power she didn't know what to do with, and didn't want.

I knew about being in love, as everybody did. I knew about it from films and novels and poetry, and although it intrigued me, I didn't long for it, or hunt it out in the way that other girls did. I couldn't imagine myself in ecstasy or despair over any of the boys I'd ever met.

Love was a word flung round corridors in our boarding houses. Girls talked about it constantly. I once said to Leila, early on, 'But how would you know? If you'd never felt it before, how would you recognise it?'

She said, 'You just would.'

•

She was right, of course, although at first I hadn't known it, because at first it was slow.

I thought about her all the time. I missed her when she was away, and then I began to miss her even when she was near me. Lying beside me on my bed, I missed her because she wasn't close enough. I longed to reach out my hand and touch her, not just her hair or her face, but all of her.

I didn't, though. I lay in bed at night and I thought, *I love her.* ***Her.*** And it shocked me.

And then I thought, *I wonder if she feels it, too.*

•

At the weekend, we shopped together for clothes. Then we came back and spent the rest of the day in our room, spread out on her rug on the floor. We drank tea and ate biscuits, and we talked.

She said, 'My father is coming tomorrow.'

I asked, 'On his own?'

'Yes.'

'Why doesn't he ever bring your sister with him?'

'She's only my half-sister.'

'But even so…'

She shrugged. 'It's because of Katherine. She doesn't trust me.'

'But you're her family. She shouldn't be deprived her of her sister. Your dad should make sure of that.'

She looked away from me. 'It's complicated.'

We were silent for a while. When she looked back at me, she said, 'I'm glad you came here.' She took my hand and held it in hers.

'I am, too.'

I didn't look at her, but I knew she was looking at me. I felt her hand leave mine and then she ran it along my side, lightly, like feathers. I shivered.

'Sssssh,' she whispered, and I wasn't sure why, because I hadn't said anything. She leaned forwards and kissed my lips.

Afterwards, she said, 'I think we can be expelled for this.'

I said, 'I don't care.'

And I didn't.

•

She was seventeen now, and I was eighteen. For three years, we'd hidden our relationship from staff and the other girls. But they'd become suspicious recently. Mrs Drew walked in one evening, and she saw us together. Even though we hadn't been doing very much, she saw enough to understand that we were more than just roommates. She reported us to the headmistress, and there was a record of it now on our files in the boarding house. It said, 'homosexual experimentation', which amused Leila and annoyed me. I found it patronising, as though what we shared was nothing more than a phase to be outgrown.

They didn't know, when they caught us and then separated us, how long it had been going on. They had no idea. Ours was a quiet love, a secret that only we knew about. Sometimes, I struggled to remember what we'd done before we met. It was hard to imagine we'd even been alive.

I used to think, If she died, and only the smallest part of her remained, I could still identify her. I would recognise a finger, a knuckle, a nail. I could run my hand over one small patch of skin, and I'd know if it were hers. They could send me her hair. I'd find her in the smell of it.

They didn't know, when they moved us to different rooms 'for our own good', that all I ever needed was to think of her. They had no idea of the memories we'd given one another, alone in our room. They'd never know, never imagine, that there were times when I barely needed to touch her. And if they'd known, they would never have understood: they couldn't separate us, not really. We didn't even need to be together.

•

On Sunday mornings, the bell woke us at nine. It was the longest we were allowed to sleep in all week. Anything else was thought of as slovenly, and a waste. Although we were in the sixth form, they still made us wear uniforms, and worse than that, on Sundays they made us wear black suits for Chapel and then stay in them all day. They never gave us any reason for this, and I could never think of any. When I asked one of the teachers once, I was merely told that it was the way things had been done here for two-hundred years and therefore it was the way they would continue to be done. But if we did everything the way they'd done it all two-hundred years ago, we'd be eating lard for breakfast and still dying of TB.

The school chapel was behind the main building. It was only used on Sundays, except by the choir, who practised there at lunchtimes, and by the Catholic girls who went to confess. Officially, Rotherfield Hall was a Catholic school, but it took in anyone, as long as their parents could pay the fees.

If we could, Leila and I would have skipped the Sunday services and spent them in bed, but we knew by now that we'd only get caught out. They'd have checked our rooms, or else counted everyone in the chapel and found us missing, and it was much easier to get away with the bigger transgressions if you stuck to the smaller rules with the willingness and obedience of angels.

We sat on a pew at the back, near the three-tiered burner where girls could leave candles as prayers, or in memory of others. When I first arrived at the school, before I'd met Leila properly, or spoken to her, I used to notice her as the girl who lit three candles on Sundays after Chapel. I wondered who they were for. I still wasn't sure about the third one. Perhaps it was meant for her.

Apart from the candles, Leila didn't like going to Chapel, and not because she wasn't spiritual, because she was in her own way. But she thought they were out to brainwash us. Their talk was generally about God's far-reaching plan and how everything that had ever happened needed to be seen as a part of that, even if we struggled to understand it. Leila thought that if that were the case, The Plan was malevolent, because as far as she could see, life was cruel and unjust. Terrible things happened to people who'd done nothing to deserve it, and all you needed to do was look at Katherine for proof of that. She said that after Alfie died, there'd been people who tried to comfort Katherine by saying God had a plan, and He loved Alfie and had taken him to a better place. Katherine broke down then, and asked how anyone could have loved him more than she had done, and what better place could there be for him than here on earth with his mother and his family?

The vicar's sermon was on the first murder. He stood at the front, telling us how Cain had risen up in a fit of jealous temper and killed his brother and soaked the ground with his blood. He preached this sermon at least once every year, unlike the others, which came around less often. Leila used to think it was because the headmistress or the school counsellor had told him what had happened, and he was directing it at her in case she really was guilty and wanted to ask forgiveness and repent and go to heaven. Since then, though, she'd decided the vicar was probably just a repressed criminal, longing for blood in the same way the housemistresses were longing for sex and cocaine.

As he preached on and on, Leila stood beside me, staring straight ahead. She looked uncomfortable. I knew she was thinking of Alfie. I had to look away from her, because whenever she was near me like that, I found it very hard not to simply reach out my hand so I had to try and focus very hard on the sermon or the others in the room. If I didn't, I'd start wishing she was naked, and really, we weren't supposed to be having those thoughts in the chapel, particularly as it had such a devout Catholic leaning.

Afterwards, we sang *Morning has Broken*, and Leila stood and moved closer to me, so our skirts were touching, and briefly, she coiled her fingers through mine. She looked at me and smiled, and as she took her hand away, my fingers brushed her skirt where it hovered over the round flesh of her backside. She glanced at me again, and I couldn't wait for the service to be over so we could have the rest of the day free.

Mrs Drew looked at us and glared, so I went back to singing and thought how good it would be when we'd finally left this school and all its rules. They were so big on purifying the spirit, but no one ever said a word about love.

Before we left the chapel, Leila lit her three tapered candles and slotted them into the burner. She always put her mother's in first, on the top level, and then Alfie's underneath at the bottom. The third she put between them. As we walked down the chapel steps and into the garden, I said, 'Who is your third candle for?'

She said, 'For all of us.'

•

My parents usually phoned on Sundays, but this week they were away. They said they sent my brother and me to boarding schools in the UK because they were better than the schools in the States, though I didn't know how they'd worked that out, having never been to a school in America themselves. I'd always known the real reason we were away at school was because my father couldn't cope with noise and my mother was the least maternal person I knew. She moved so quickly, there wasn't a hope of a child keeping up with her, and she never waited for anyone. They also wanted us both to become politicians or barristers, and seemed certain that sleeping at school and being cared for by emotionally defective housemistresses was a necessary stepping stone towards such a career. They might have been right, but their noble plans still failed. My brother was twenty-one, and currently a smack addict in South London.

They didn't know about Leila, although I'd often thought about telling them, for the shock factor if nothing else. Deviant sexuality was not high on their list of wishes for their offspring's achievements. They'd have preferred me to win a cup for public speaking.

They were pleased – or perhaps relieved – that I was going to university, even if it wasn't Oxbridge. They were less happy with my choice of subject, which was Psychology. My mother was against Psychology as a discipline. For a start, it was too new, and she certainly didn't want me to pursue it as a career. She felt very strongly that people needed to learn to live without being propped up by others all the time, which had always amused me – she overlooked the fact that my father's money was the only thing keeping her alive.

After Chapel, Leila and I went to our rooms to gather our pens and books. Because it was warm outside and the sun was shining, we took them over to the top lawn. The top lawn was only for the sixth form girls. It had tables and chairs and parasols, so we could study there in good weather. Although it was the weekend and lots of the others had gone home, the ones who were left had had the same idea as us, and the grass was covered with groups of girls in black suits, their skirts rolled up to the tops of their legs so they could lounge about in them more comfortably. If any dubious characters from outside were hidden among the trees, watching, they'd have been at least moderately satisfied.

Leila had brought a blanket from her room, which she spread over the ground beneath the horse chestnut tree in the farthest corner. We laid down on it, side by side on our fronts. I took out my French book and tried to read, but it was boring and I couldn't concentrate. Leila was much better at studying than me. She loved it. That was why she always did so well. It was one thing to be able to understand things, but another to understand them passionately in the way that she did. Sometimes, though she never told anyone, I knew she cried in secret over the poems in our English anthologies.

A single magpie scratched at the grass in front of us. Leila lifter her eyes from her book and saluted it. 'Good morning, Mr Magpie,' she said, and although I'd never been a superstitious person myself, I couldn't blame her, as she'd had enough of sorrow and bad luck.

She turned to me and said, 'I'm going to ask my father to let us go back for the summer, like we planned. Katherine will just have to live with it. My father *wants* me to go home. He said he did.'

There was heat in her words. I said, 'Do you think they'll agree?'

'I hope so.'

It was what I hoped, too, and not just because we'd be able to spend the summer together as we'd planned, but because Leila deserved a home. When she first came to school, her father had said it was only going to be for three months or so, just while Katherine recovered from losing Alfie. But it had been eight years now, and she was still here.

She picked up her book again, and the moment for talking was past. There were parts of her life that I would always be shut out of. She didn't talk about what happened very often, but still it hung there like an old sky, and if I wanted to share her world, then I had to live under it, too.

•

Later in the evening, when we were drinking wine in our room and our conversation had drifted back to Katherine and the new baby, I said, 'Do you think she's losing her mind?'

Leila laughed. 'Probably. I don't know whether my father even wants any more children. He's nearly fifty.'

I knew Katherine was much younger, still only in her early thirties.

She moved back to the window and lit a cigarette. 'Maybe she's done it to try and keep my father at home more.' She shrugged, 'To stop him from coming here to see me.'

She sounded dejected. I didn't know what to do. I knew that if I put my arms around her, she'd probably cry, and she hated crying in front of people. She preferred them all to think she was invincible. Hardly anyone saw in her the qualities that I did, but if they'd just taken a moment, I knew they would have done. Her qualities were obvious, once you got near.

I stood up and carried our empty glasses back to the wardrobe. We weren't supposed to keep anything from the kitchen in our rooms, so we needed to hide the few things we did have. There were times, I thought, when permanent Girl Guide camp would have been easier than boarding school. At least at camp, you could keep everything you needed close by, and thirst was generally accepted as part of the human condition.

I stuck a cork in the wine bottle and hid it under my bed, along with the empty bottles that needed recycling. None of the girls here were allowed to bring cars, even if they'd passed their driving tests, so we had to carry one bottle at a time, concealed under our jackets or in our bags. Very often, they'd stand at the gates and search us as we went out. Lots of girls got caught in that way. Usually their bottles were full and then they'd have to stay inside for a month. I didn't know what the punishment would have been for carrying an empty bottle into town, but I was sure they'd think of something.

She stood at the window with her back to me. I couldn't tell what she was thinking.

She pulled the curtains and came away from the window. I wondered whether she might go back to her own room. She did that occasionally. Although on most nights, we curled into one bed and zipped ourselves up spine to spine, there were other times when we just needed to spread out by ourselves and sleep, so she'd go to her room and I'd stay in mine. As much as anything, it was a way of letting the housemistresses think we were listening to them.

I took a chair away from the desk and propped it against the door. We didn't have locks, and weren't supposed to block the staff out or they'd automatically have become even more suspicious. A chair would never have stopped the door from being opened, but at least it bought us some time.

When I turned round again, she was sitting on my bed. She smiled. 'Sit by me.'

We were silent for a while, and I took her hand.

She said, 'It doesn't matter if we can't go back there in the summer. We'll just have to find somewhere else instead. We could go away, get jobs.'

I smiled, relieved, and she put her arms around me, and then her lips swept mine, briefly, softly. They were warm. She pulled away, and touched my face with her fingers, trailing them down my cheek to my throat. Our eyes met and locked. *I love you,* she whispered. It was so soft I could barely hear it, but I kept it, and remembered it.

She put her mouth to mine. Our lips parted and our tongues touched, and she stroked her palm slowly over the back of my neck. As we kissed, she pulled me down on the bed with her. We faced each other sideways, and our hands felt their way under jumpers and jeans, searching for the skin we hadn't seen or touched since the morning.

I untied her top and traced my fingers over the white arc of her stomach. She lied beneath me, raising my t-shirt up over my head and unbuttoning my jeans, which I twisted out of. Beneath her bra, I could see the round flesh of her breasts. I unhooked it and drop it to the floor, and for a moment I stopped and looked, and thought how exquisite her body was, and it made my breath come faster, until all I wanted was to touch all of her.

I started sliding her skirt off over her hips, and moved my hands up and down the inside of her thigh as I did. She shivered a little, and when her skirt was off, and as my fingers moved upwards against her skin again, I heard her: a brief, tiny moan, and I found the very top of her thigh was wet, and so I moved down to kiss it. I had the taste of her then on my lips, and she was almost naked beside me, except for the white lace of the thong that veiled the small strip of hair underneath. The lace was soaked as I peeled it away from her, and it made me so happy I gasped. She arched her back.

Please, she murmured.

I slipped two fingers there, where she wanted them, and then after a while I slid them, gently, under and into her, and she began to gasp. As I circled my fingers inside her, I lowered my mouth to the soft pink of her flesh, and moved my tongue over and over her, until she could barely lie still and then she cried out, loudly and urgently, and I slowed down, and then stopped.

She gathered me back up towards her and wrapped her arms around me, and we lay there silently together. Then, after a while, she turned her face towards me, fit her lips to mine, and moved her tongue back into my mouth. I closed my eyes and felt her hand caressing my face and then my stomach, and slowly moving down until finally she rose above me and lowered her thighs to mine. She searched for my gaze. I looked back at her, and kissed her, and I raised my hips and began to move them with her and against her, and I knew, even though I was only just eighteen, that I would never love anyone else like this again, and I didn't want to, and afterwards it was these thoughts, because they were so strong and not because they were sad, that made me cry.

•

Just after ten-thirty, someone knocked on my door. We were both wearing pyjamas by then, and sitting innocently on the floor, playing cards. Neither of us particularly liked cards, unless it was poker and we played against the other girls for money. It was simply that we had to use up some of our time in a wholesome way, or they'd have watched us even more closely. If they'd separated us permanently, it would have made our lives unbearable, agonising. So we played cards to pass the time, until we knew it was safe to go to bed again.

I'd already moved the chair away from the door. It opened straight away. Mrs Drew stood in the doorway and looked around. 'Right, Leila. Time to go to your own room, please.'

Everyone hated Mrs Drew. Although all the housemistresses would have dismally failed a personality test, she was the worst of the lot. Her face was pale, like eggshell, which was probably why she hardly smiled – in case it broke and she was left without one, although it's possible that no face at all would have been a vast improvement on the one she had. It was no surprise that she was so miserable. After all, she'd sacrificed her days and nights of freedom for life in a girls' boarding school, where her entire reason for living seemed to be making sure that countless pairs of female legs stayed bound together until the day we sat our last exam. Her own, at least, carried a guarantee – and no doubt for a lifetime.

Leila ignored her.

'Leila, did you hear what I said?'

'Yes, Mrs Drew. I heard what you said.'

'Well, are you planning to move, or not?'

'Yes, Mrs Drew. I'm planning to move.'

'Now?'

'In a moment, Mrs Drew, when I'm ready.'

'I am asking you to leave now, Leila.'

Leila continued to sit with her back to her. She picked another card. 'Fuck,' she said, when she looked at it.

'If you leave now, Leila, I will pretend not have heard that. If you stay any longer, I won't. And I will also,' she added, 'begin to notice the disgusting smell of cigarettes in this room.'

Leila threw her cards down on the floor. 'Oh, for God's sake. I'll go.' And then, right in front of Mrs Drew, she leaned forwards and kissed me, smash on the mouth. Even though I knew she'd done it for Mrs Drew's benefit, there was still a tenderness to that kiss that made it impossible for me to imagine she could ever have laid a finger on anyone, in anything other than love.

V

Leila

Betrayal was the worst sin. My mother didn't want her there. I knew that, even though I had no proof.

They went out together and left me alone. I searched their room. It used to be my father's. Now it was both of theirs, and I wasn't allowed in.

I was looking for my mother. She used to be in there, hidden in all the boxes in his wardrobe that he never let me open. I knew that was where she was and I wanted to see if he'd kept her, despite Katherine. He hadn't. He'd hidden her away in the cellar, in the room where no one went.

They called it Letting Go. The final stage of grief. No one got to that point with Alfie. They all got stuck at Stage Two. Searching.

I left their room and went down to the cellar. It had always frightened me. It was a forbidden place, but I knew where the key was. My father hid it behind a loose brick in the wall.

I took the key and pulled open the door. My nose filled with dusty air.

I stood at the top of the cement stairway that disappeared down to the dark mouth of the cellar beneath. There was a light somewhere. I groped until my fingers found a switch, and then all of a sudden the air and the steps glowed red. I stepped down, further into the darkness.

At the bottom, I stopped. Strange shapes were waiting for me in the red glow.

Dusty wine racks, cardboard boxes, old furniture covered in plastic sheets. I was under the house and underground, caught in the hum of the earth. The cellar walls sweated and dripped. They were grey and cracked and decayed, as though they'd tried to split themselves open, then given up and started rotting away.

I closed my eyes. I had a memory of coming down here once after my mother had died, and finding rotten apples. Maybe they were still there, sweet and mouldy and creeping with worms.

Propped up against the wall, under a plastic sheet, were long sections of carved wood. I peered through the plastic, and saw sheets of paper sellotaped to them. *Assembling your baby's cot.*

On the ground beside the cot were boxes. I knelt down and rummaged through them, until I found one that just said *Elizabeth.*

I opened it.

A red velvet case. Inside, a gold ring.

A book. *Wedding.* It was bursting with photos. My mother in a white dress, standing outside the church with my father when he was young.

An envelope. Two letters.

Another book. Old and battered. *The Cookery Year.*

Odd pieces of paper with blue writing. Shopping lists or Christmas lists. *Dolls' house, paddling pool, velvet dress.*

A pink leaflet: *St Michael's Church, September 25th. A Celebration of the life of Elizabeth Hartley. Order of Service.*

And a page from the local newspaper

I put everything back, except the newspaper and a photo from the wedding album. I looked around. There was another box. *Leila. Baby*

Souvenirs. The handwriting was my mother's. It was the same as the writing on the lists, and on the back of the photo I kept in my secret chest.

The box had an album in it, and another book with pages of information. Weight at birth: 6lb, 12oz. First real tears: 12 weeks, 3 days. First tooth: 11 months. First step: 13 months. First word: 11 months.

There were other things in there, too. A lock of fine black baby hair wrapped in tissue, a tiny pair of jeans, fluffy slippers, a tooth. All of them kept together in the cellar, like the hidden remains of some gruesome infant murder.

I picked up the newspaper page and the envelope, and ran away out of the cellar, back upstairs to my room.

•

That afternoon, I hid.

I took the old doll I'd found in the basket on my bike, and crept among the fir trees at the side of the garden, squeezing myself behind a tree trunk. I was a hedgehog, a woodlouse, a long spotted snake that could disguise itself in the dirt and spit clear arcs of poison at anyone who came near.

The back door opened. I held my breath.

'Leila!'

I was supposed to be staying at Rosie's. My father was going out with people from work. They had to stay over in London. That was what he told me. But I knew he was going away with Katherine.

'Leila!'

I stayed quiet. I sat the doll on my lap and began to plait the strands of her hair. She was still dirty from all that time in the barn.

My father was getting nearer. I heard his feet breaking twigs on the ground, and the rustle of leaves as he pushed through the trees and poked his head inside the hollow.

'Come on. We'll be late.'

I still said nothing. A thick brown slug trailed over the grass towards the undergrowth at the back. I edged away from it.

'Leila!'

His voice was sharper now. I stood up. 'I don't want to go.'

'It's only for one night. I thought you liked staying at Rosie's.'

I shrugged. *Not always,* I thought. *Not always.* 'Why can't I go another day instead?'

He sighed. 'We've been through this already. Come on.'

I abandoned the doll on the ground and crawled out from under the trees to the garden. A stone stuck in my knee and left a dent in my skin when I picked it off. My father took my hand and we crossed the garden to the gate at the side. I could see Rosie's oast house from there. The front was round, like a giant tower.

We walked up to the front door and my father rang the bell. He looked down at me and ruffled my hair, the way my mother sometimes did. Except she didn't ruffle. She only stroked.

Come, she said.

•

We went upstairs to Rosie's room. She had her own double bed. She had a karaoke machine, and as soon as we got upstairs, she turned it on and pretended to be a famous singer. She was a good singer. She wanted to go on stage.

At the end of the song, she was breathless. She passed the microphone to me.

'There you are. Your turn.'

I said, 'I don't want to.'

'Why not?'

'I just don't.'

Rosie dropped the microphone on the carpet and flopped onto her bed. 'Your house is for sale.'

'I know.'

A group of men had come last week and put a sign up in the front garden. *For Sale*. My father and Katherine wanted a house of their own. I knew what that meant. A house free of my mother.

'Where are you going?'

'I don't know. Africa.'

'Liar. I bet Katherine's coming to live with you.'

I was quiet.

'Is she, then?'

'Yeah.'

'Do you think they do it?'

'What?'

'You know. *It*.'

I knew. I said, 'No. They definitely don't.'

'I bet they do. Alison – that's my mum – thinks Katherine's having a baby.'

'She is not.'

'She is. She's getting really fat.'

I tried to remember the last time I'd seen Katherine. I couldn't remember her being fat.

'What would you do if she is?'

'I don't know. But she isn't.'

Rosie lowered her voice. 'If my mum and dad had their own baby, they'd send me back to the children's home.'

'They wouldn't. They wouldn't be allowed.'

'They would. No one wants kids that aren't theirs. Not when they've got their own. You'll have to watch out, if Katherine *is* pregnant. She definitely won't want you then.'

I looked at the carpet. Perhaps she was right.

•

At night, we slept in her double bed.

It was raining outside. I told Rosie about my mother coming to me at night.

She didn't respond, but she was thinking about it. I knew that.

She told me then about the children's home she'd been in. Lots of people lived there. The children didn't usually stay for long. They got thrown out, or ran away, or killed themselves. The staff didn't stay, either. The job was too hard. They didn't care enough, or they cared too much.

She went quiet for a while. Then she said, 'My real parents aren't really rich and famous like I said they were.'

I'd guessed that already. I said, 'What were they, then?'

'My dad's in prison. I don't know where my mum is. I think she went crazy.'

There was a strange hooked sound when she spoke, like her voice had been caught round barbed wire.

As I listened to her, it felt as if she'd come from somewhere far, far away, and as if she were years and years older, not just two years. She'd taken a one-way trip, and looked into the world of adults. She could never come back.

I said, 'Did you like your real mum and dad?'

'No.' She was silent for a moment, then she laughed. 'No. They were real pieces of shit.'

•

Rosie fell asleep. It was late. Her father was away, but I heard Alison coming to bed.

Whenever I closed my eyes, I could see the page from the newspaper that I'd found in the cellar. I'd read it so many times, I knew all the words by heart. They made me angry. No one had ever told me, and I couldn't remember.

I couldn't remember.

21st February

A man will appear in the Crown Court next Thursday afternoon, faced with a charge of causing death by dangerous driving.

On September 16th last year, Elizabeth Hartley, 35, was killed when Ian

Rowe's Toyota MR2 ploughed into the side of her Fiat Uno at nearly 60 mph in a 30mph zone. Her unborn child, who had been due in November, also died. Her daughter Leila, 5, was with her, but escaped with minor injuries.

A local man who assisted at the scene of the accident told police Rowe was driving 'like a lunatic.'

It is not yet known for certain whether alcohol played a part in the crash.

Rowe, 52, has one previous conviction for dangerous driving.

I kept looking at the ceiling. I couldn't remember the accident. I hadn't known there was a baby.

VI

Olivia

We'd had the best spring for years. Nearly every day, the sky had been out, and it kept the sea blue and took the edge of it when we swam at night. Like most things, night swimming was forbidden, but we found ways round that. We loved the sea and the dark together. They hid us.

It was Sunday morning. We were in Leila's room at the top of the building. She stubbed out her cigarette on the window ledge and tossed the end onto the roof outside. It was so close to the end of term now, she didn't care anymore who caught her. She left the window open so the room would air while we were out.

She picked her bag up from the floor. It was small and hand-stitched with beads and sequins, and everyone admired it. She had a knack for finding pretty things. She dressed perfectly and always looked like a sculpture or a queen, even if she was only wearing jeans.

'Ready?' she asked.

I smiled. 'Yes.'

Before she opened the door she stood on her tiptoes and kissed me suddenly, and for a long time. Her lips were deep brown and glossy. They tasted sweet, like chocolate. When she pulled away, she said, 'Thank you for doing this.'

'I want to,' I said.

We walked down the corridor and the back staircases to the bottom of the main house. A few girls were wandering about in their dressing gowns, carrying magazines or cups of tea, but it wasn't really very busy. Most were still in bed, even though we were supposed to use our Saturday mornings now for revision. Hardly anyone did, not even Leila, and she was the hardest working of anyone I knew. Lots of people found that strange, because Leila was bound to do well, no matter what, and she'd taken the entrance exam to Oxford so barely even needed to pass her A Levels. But she was a perfectionist. I'd never seen anything like it.

At the bottom of the stairs in the entrance hall was a small wooden table with a book we were supposed to sign to tell the housemistresses where we were going. That was their idea of a sixth-form privilege – the fact that we no longer had to ask to leave the school grounds on a Saturday. Leila refused to do it. It offended her to be kept track of like that, as though we were inmates in a prison, or lunatics that couldn't be trusted to walk round Eastbourne by ourselves. The irony of it was that there really wasn't anywhere to go, so keeping track of us was barely worthwhile. No one ever got into trouble in Eastbourne, except for those tortured souls who flung themselves from Beachy Head. Leila once said she could understand them, which frightened me for a moment, but all she meant was that she understood why they would travel from all over the country just to do it. She thought the splendour of the drop would take some of the pain away, and it would be a much pleasanter fall than one from a tower block in Newcastle. You'd feel closer to heaven, at least, except, of course, you'd be going in the wrong direction.

Once we were out of sight of the school, she took my hand again. She said, 'Katherine was going to come with my father today, but he phoned to say she can't make it. Grace is sick.'

'Is that just an excuse, do you think?'

She shrugged. 'Possibly.'

I'd never met any of Leila's family, not even her father, though I'd seen him lots of times from a distance. Katherine and the two girls were the reason why Leila hardly ever went home. Until now, Katherine would only let her go back when it was absolutely necessary, and that usually just meant Christmas, because it was hard to find guardians who were willing to take anyone in then. So that was the time, Leila said, when her father put his foot down. I personally had always thought he should put his foot down more often, though Leila said there was no point, as she didn't want to see Katherine any more than Katherine wanted to see her, and that was just the way it was always going to be.

We walked across the fields that ran over the cliff tops. They were full of families and dog-walkers. Lots of people smiled at us as we passed them, perhaps because we looked like sweet young friends, or perhaps just to show that they were liberal-minded.

I said to Leila, 'Does your father know about us?'

She shook her head. 'I don't know. I don't think so. Even if he suspected, he'd never ask me. Never.'

'Do you think he'd mind if he did know?'

'Not really. He'd be relieved that no man was coming me.'

I laughed. It was probably the way my own father would feel, too, although my mother was a different matter.

I said, 'But we'll have to hide it from him, when we're in their house.'

'Maybe.'

We carried on walking. The wind blew the hair away from her face, and the sun caught the chain around her neck. I said, 'You're still wearing your mother's ring.'

Quickly, she lifted her hair and asked me to unclasp it. She dropped the chain into the pocket inside her bag. 'I'm not sure what my father would say if he knew I had this.'

'Do you think he hasn't realised? It's been gone for nearly eight years.'

She paused for a moment and seemed to think about it, then said, 'He might not have done. Katherine hardly lets him acknowledge that he was married before she came along. He probably hasn't been near my mother's things since before I came to school.'

She stayed silent as we followed the road down to the village. Far ahead of us, the sea swayed to the horizon. She said, 'Oh God, I hope you'll like him.'

She sounded so anxious suddenly I laughed. 'Of course I will.' And then, to reassure her, I said, 'But it doesn't matter if I don't.'

'You know, it isn't him,' she said slowly. 'It isn't him. It's her. It's her and her fucking children.'

I glanced at her as we walked. Her face had hardened. I knew, when she was like this, that I couldn't reach her, and there was nothing I could say. It was him. Of course it was him. He was her father. He'd made the wrong choice.

•

We arrived before he did. The café was on the seafront, and dimly lit inside. It was in the area of town known as 'up-and-coming', which really just meant it had spotlights in the ceiling instead of the dark brown lampshades that were hangovers from a more socially deprived era, which nowhere in Eastbourne had yet brought itself to abandon.

Leila ordered drinks. We took them outside and sat at wooden tables on the terrace overlooking the beach. She was nervous and uncomfortable. Her eyes were darting in any of the directions she thought he might come from.

She sucked her drink up through a straw and said, 'Keep watching out for him. He looks like me. He's me in drag.'

'I've seen him before.'

She didn't listen. She shielded her eyes from the sun and looked westwards down the street. 'There he is. That's him,' she said. She stood up, and straightened her skirt, and fumbled with the buttons on her cardigan.

I watched as he approached. He hadn't seen us. He looked sombre at first, and although I'd heard the expression about people's faces lighting up when they saw someone, I'd always thought it was just a cliché or a figure of speech. But when he came closer, that was exactly what happened. He beamed at Leila, and his eyes shone and he started to run.

I felt intrusive. I pretended not to notice that she stood there stiffly and didn't return his embrace.

He sat down, and shook my hand and smiled. 'You must be Olivia. I'm pleased to meet you. Leila talks about you all the time.'

I smiled. He had brown hair and a beard that no doubt used to be brown but was now grey. It was the sort of beard that made a man look warm and approachable.

I thought his eyes were sad, but possibly I was imagining that.

He handed Leila a black carrier bag with curly lettering on it. 'I found them in an antique bookshop in London last week,' he said. He looked at her as she opened it, as though he were handing her the moon.

She brought out a leather bound book. She held it out in front of her for a moment, then turned it over. Its cover was crimson with a gold leaf boarder. *Little Women*.

She faltered. 'Thanks, dad.'

He leant back in his chair and smiled. 'They had the whole series. I bought them all. I know you've already got them, but those are just old paperbacks…' He shrugged as he saw Leila's face, and trailed off, and looked embarrassed.

She reached out and touched his arm. 'They're great, dad. Thank you.'

He smiled again, relieved. 'Ok. I know you're probably too old for them, but they're classics.' He glanced inside at the bar. 'I'll get some drinks.'

He hurried off. Leila turned to me, and looked sad. 'These books were my favourites when I still lived at home. I made him read them to me over and over in the months after Alfie died. He's remembered. Even though it was years ago, he still thinks they're my favourites.' She paused, and took a second book out of the bag. It matched the first. She ran her fingers gently over the spine. 'I don't know whether this is really sad, or just sweet of him. He can't have discussed it with Katherine. She'd have said I was too old, and talked him out of it.'

And for that reason, I think, the books became precious to her.

•

We ordered lunch. Sometimes, as we were talking, I could see him looking at us curiously and I thought, *He knows.* But he was friendly to me, and I wondered whether he liked the fact that Leila had met someone she cared about.

She smoked one cigarette after another. We talked about nothing with any meaning, and as the time passed, I grew sad for Leila and Gus, because the day had an aimless feel to it, as though neither of them really knew what they should be doing, and because the weight of so many unsaid words kept hanging between them.

Eventually, Gus said, 'Katherine and the girls are really looking forward to having you to stay for the summer.' It was obvious what an effort it had been, just for him to broach the subject like that.

Leila gave a short sigh. 'Good.'

He fell silent, and looked at the table.

I'd asked Leila once about Katherine, and why he was still living with someone who made his life so difficult. I didn't think she really knew or understood. She thought it was because he wanted a family, and that having them was better than not having them. And he didn't want to be separated from anymore of his children. He lost his whole family when her mother died. Her grandmother had told Leila that they'd tried and tried for another baby after she was born, but it wasn't until she was five that her mother became pregnant again, but then all of a sudden there was a car crash, and she was dead before the baby had even been born. It always seemed so strange and awful to me how that could happen – simple, everyday lives plunged into all the agony of sorrow and chaos in a moment.

He brightened his tone and said, 'You're welcome to stay for as long as you want to, Olivia. The whole holiday if you need to.'

'Thank you.' I glanced at Leila. 'I know my mother would like me to join them in New York for a few weeks. I thought I might leave after the baby is born, so you can the time with your family.'

Leila looked shocked and hurt. I'd never discussed it with her, and I didn't really mean it. It was something to say, to be polite. I kicked her under the table, and smiled.

Gus shook his head. 'It's fine. The house is big enough, and Leila will be bored over the summer otherwise, with just me and Katherine, and two small girls and a baby to fill her time.'

The only time I'd spoken about it with Leila, she'd said that everything in her family was always so close to falling apart, any serious change would unhinge it completely. If I went with her, her presence in the house would be diluted and she'd be less like part of the family and more like a guest, though much easier than a welcome guest as she wouldn't need any looking after.

Gus cleared his throat. When he spoke, he didn't look at either of us. He said, 'Rosie will be back next door when you come home, Leila.'

She looked up. Her voice was abrupt and sharp. 'How do you know?'

'I saw her mother the other day. Rosie's been living in London these last few years. She's broke now, and in debt. She didn't tell anyone about it. I think she's in quite serious trouble. That's why she's having to come home. To lick her wounds.'

Leila nodded, and moved the food around her plate without eating any of it.

Gus continued. 'And Katherine had a scan the other week. I didn't tell you last time I saw you, but we're expecting another boy.'

Leila gave a short laugh, like glass breaking. 'That's nice,' she said.

Another boy, I thought, *like a collection, except that the first one was lost.*

•

Later in the evening, when he'd dropped us back at school, we locked ourselves in the bathroom farthest away down the corridor that led to the fire escape at the back of the boarding house. The bath in there was ancient, and the water coming out of the taps rusty at first. No one used it, except us. But it was away from the main building, and that was all we cared about.

I undressed and climbed in while Leila rolled up a towel and blocked it against the gap under the door. She opened a window, then lit a cigarette and put a glass on the edge of the bath for an ashtray.

I watched her and said, 'For a posh girl, you're very squalid.'

She smiled. 'For a posh girl, you're very tolerant.'

She came into the bath and lay with her back against me. She breathed in on her cigarette. 'Sorry if things were awkward today.'

'They were fine.'

She paused, then looked up at me and said, 'Did you mean what you said about leaving when the baby's born?'

I hesitated for a moment. 'I'm not sure. It just seems strange, to intrude on a family like that.'

'You won't be intruding. We're not close. We all hate each other.' She laughed. 'The house is big. They'll be busy. They'll hardly notice us. And I can't bear the thought of you in America while I'm here. The distance is too much.'

I filled my palms with soap and swept them over her back. 'I know.'

'Then stay.'

'I'd like to.'

We sat in silence while she finished her cigarette. She stubbed it out, then turned over to face me, her legs and hips close against mine. She lowered her mouth to my lips, and moved her tongue over my tongue, and we kissed slowly, for a long time.

'I love you.'

'I love you.'

The water splashed us then, and I leant further back and raised my hips as her legs parted and she began to move, up and then down against me.

Our eyes met. She pushed wet hair from my face.

'Stay,' she said again.

VII

Leila

My father's birthday. I'd saved my pocket money for weeks. I counted it. I hid it so no one would find it if they came to the house and broke in.

Katherine said she'd take me shopping. She picked me up from school and took me home. We waited there for Rosie. Rosie's school was in the next village.

There'd been no room at mine when she moved in.

From the kitchen window, I could see her walking up the garden path. She was wearing lipstick, pink and glossy. She had breasts. They were tiny, but they were definitely there. She was proud of them. She showed them off. 'You can touch them if you want,' she said once. But I didn't, not then.

She came in. She gave Katherine a bunch of flowers. Katherine was pleased.

She loved flowers back then. They were beautiful and pure, untouched by the howling of grief.

Katherine liked Rosie. All the adults did. They said she was mature. She was. She knew about men, and women, and what you had to do. She told me. Later, much later, she showed me.

Katherine dropped the flowers in a vase. Rosie stood with her back against the worktop. She stared at Katherine's stomach, and elbowed me in the ribs. She pointed one finger. I looked. Beneath Katherine's jumper and black trousers, I made it out: a small round shape. A baby.

It was the first time I saw Alfie, and I didn't want him there.

•

The shopping centre was quiet. There were mainly teenagers from the secondary schools, standing around outside, smoking cigarettes, talking in loud voices.

We headed to a department store that had a gift section for men. I found a water resistant radio for the shower. I wanted to buy it. I knew my father would like it. It was in the shape of a dolphin and I thought it would make him laugh. Katherine was busy in another aisle, looking at things for the kitchen, planning her new home. I picked the radio up and took it to the counter.

I stood at the back of the queue behind an old woman. Rosie came over and said, 'Katherine just told me we can go off by ourselves for twenty minutes. She said I can take you to look in the toy shop, but you have to stay with me all the time.'

I said, 'I have to pay for this.'

Rosie shook her head. 'Pay later. Let's go.'

She took the radio out of my hand and left it on the wrong shelf as we walked out of the shop.

•

The toyshop was on the next floor up. I didn't play with toys by then, except for the broken dolls the woman brought me at school. I only played with those because I had to, because my father was paying her, so she could access my mind and assess it. But it wasn't that easy. I kept her guessing. I kept them all guessing, forever. Not Olivia, though. I told Olivia.

Rosie was acting older again. She always did that in public, when people could hear her. 'What toy would you like, Leila?'

I ignored her and walked away to another aisle. They had a basket full of tiny dolls with silver wings, like fairies or angels. I picked one up. It had golden hair to its toes, like my mother always did in my dreams. I decided to buy it, and keep it by my bed.

Rosie had disappeared. There was a room at the back of the shop full of things for babies. I paid for the doll and went in there to find her.

She was carrying a pair of woollen baby socks in her hand. 'Look,' she said. 'Aren't they sweet?'

I nodded. 'Has it been twenty minutes yet?'

Rosie checked her watch. 'No. Only ten. I'm going to buy something for Katherine.'

'Why?'

'Because she's having a baby, stupid.'

'She might not be.'

'Of course she is. You must know why she hasn't told you about it.'

'No.'

She looked around the shop to make sure no one was listening. 'It's all part of her plan.'

'What plan?'

Rosie rolled her eyes. 'I told you. It's because she wants your dad all to herself, to start a new family with him. To do that, she needs to get rid of you. That's why she hasn't told you about the baby.'

I nodded.

Rosie held up the socks. 'So we need to get her these, just to let her know we've sussed her out and we know about it. That way, she'll soon realise she's not as clever as she thinks she is.'

'OK.'

She put her arm around me as we went to the counter. 'It's all right. I'll give them to her. You don't need to do anything.'

•

My fairy doll was wrapped up in a small paper bag. I clasped my palm around it as we walked out of the shop to meet Katherine.

I was about to step on the escalator, but a man in a black uniform came up to me. 'Hello there,' he said. 'Are you Rosie Ash?'

I shook my head. Rosie stepped in front of me. 'I'm Rosie Ash. Is there a problem?'

I knew we were in trouble. The man looked at a piece of paper in his hand, and spoke only to Rosie. 'Is this one Leila?'

Rosie nodded and he said, 'Well, Leila's mother is frantically looking for you two. Come with me.'

He led us away from the escalator, to a desk in the middle of the shopping centre. There were three other men, all wearing the same uniforms. They stared at us. He said, 'I've got them.' Another man shook his head and walked off.

The man who'd found us made us sit and wait. I unwrapped the doll from its packet and coiled its hair around my finger. It was soft on my skin.

Come.

After a while, the other man came back. Katherine was with him. She looked pale and worried. She ran up to us, and wrapped her arms around us. I stiffened. I didn't hug her back.

'Where on earth have you girls been?' Her voice shook. I knew she was going to cry.

Rosie spoke first. She stepped down from her chair. 'I'm sorry, Katherine. I'm so sorry we worried you, but you said it would be OK.'

Katherine looked at her. 'I said what would be OK, Rosie?'

'You said it was OK for me to take Leila to the toyshop. You said we could have twenty minutes, and look, it's only been fifteen.' She held out her watch for Katherine to see.

'No, I…' Katherine looked back at me, then walked over to the men. 'I'm sorry we've caused all this trouble.'

They all looked at her. She blushed.

She shook her head. 'I'm so sorry.'

One of them smiled. 'Don't worry about it. They're a nightmare, kids. A bloody nightmare.'

I never knew who told the truth that day. It was probably Katherine, but at the time, I believed Rosie.

•

11.54

I had no blind, and no curtains. Night curled into my room through the gaps at the edge of the skylight. Half a moon glowed in the distance. Another dead face.

The attic was full of faces and trees. They grew all around me, coming up close and then fading back into the walls. My father's words came and went, sliding around my head in the dark.

There were lots of words, but they all amounted to the same thing: she was pregnant. They'd shown me a photo of the baby. It looked like a fish.

I sat up and turned the light on. The words and the trees and the faces disappeared. I wrapped my arms tight around my knees.

On the floor by my bed was my old doll. I leaned over and picked her up. I shook her. Her eyes rolled. I shook her again. She was dead.

I dropped her on the duvet, then climbed out of bed and unlocked my secret chest. Inside it now were the things I'd taken from the cellar. There was also Katherine's scan photo. I'd stolen it from the pinboard in the kitchen. She didn't know. She knew it had gone, but she didn't know it was me. Or maybe she did know, but was too afraid to say. My father would never believe her.

I took the scan photo out of the secret chest and laid it on the bed by my doll, then went over to my desk, picked up some scissors and paper, and got back into bed. Very slowly, I cut the ends of the doll's hair and watched as it fell down onto the covers. I stood her up on the sheet in front of me. She didn't look very different, so I cut some more, all around her neck and close to the top of her head. When I'd finished, she was nearly bald, apart from some short blonde spikes. I trimmed the tips of her eyelashes.

I opened the drawer in my bedside table and rifled through it until I found my Jemima Puddleduck mirror. I held it up and stared at my reflection. My hair was untidy from sleep. I tilted my head to the side and cut some of my own hair away. It mingled with the doll's, and made a mess on the bed.

I pulled back the corner of the cover, knelt down on the floor and swept all the hair into my hands, then piled it neatly in the middle of a sheet of paper, wrapped it up, and wedged it into the side of my secret chest.

I looked back at the doll, lying on the bed, and gathered her into my arms. I unbuttoned her dress and laid her down on the floor. Under my bed was a plastic bag full of dolls' things. From inside it, I took a white pillow for her head, and a sheet that I wrapped round her legs. I reached for the scissors again, knelt down on the rug and bent over her. Then I opened out the scissors as far as they would go, and stabbed them into her stomach.

I pushed them in further, cutting a rough line all the way down the front of her body. Then I picked up the photo of Katherine's baby from the bed, folded it in half, and slipped it inside the hole in her stomach.

There was some sellotape on my desk that I used to mend the cut. Then I dressed the doll in her old clothes, wrapped her back up in the sheet, and laid her under the bed.

Tomorrow, I would bury her.

Part Two

I

'There,' Katherine said, and pointed. 'Just put them down there, sweetheart.'

She brushed the hair away from her face and stepped back from her daughter, heavy and exhausted. Summer had come too early this year, rolling in around March and bringing with it insects and rot. Instead of leaving after three days as everyone assumed it would, it stayed on and on, and then grew fiercer.

Holding Lily's hand, she watched as Grace kneeled down and arranged her flowers in the stone pot that formed part of Alfie's grave. Six months after he died, they'd paid extra to have it built at the base of the headstone. It collected rainwater that turned stagnant if left too long. The smell made her stomach turn, and caused more guilt. Not only had she failed to protect him from death, she now neglected him, too.

Grace stood up again, brushing the dirt from her knees. She was not a child who relished mud, or sand, or anything that stuck to her skin.

She gazed critically at the flowers for some time. Finally, she looked up at Katherine and said, 'I think he'll like them.'

Katherine smiled. 'I think so, too.'

She lifted a protesting Lily off the ground, put her in the pushchair and strapped her in. Lily kicked and cried – she preferred to walk – but the only way to get home now was to bear it.

'Come on,' she said, and held out her hand to Grace.

They walked to the cemetery gates and left him. He'd be eight now. Katherine followed his growth in other children, always on the lookout for the one who looked like Alfie. She wasn't sure what she'd do if she ever found him. Once she'd followed a woman who checked in at Heathrow airport ahead of her, certain that the boy on her arm was really hers. She'd done the same thing in Waitrose twice. Both times, she talked herself out of the madness of action, but didn't trust herself to be able to do it forever. She imagined Alfie to be brown-haired like his father, and short and pale. She thought of him with glasses. She thought of him as vulnerable.

As they turned out onto the road, Grace held the edge of the pushchair and said, 'Sometimes I really miss him.'

'I know you do,' Katherine said, and ran her fingers lightly through Grace's hair. Her child's words left a chill, like water, in her stomach. She stopped and turned her head and looked away for a moment. Gus disapproved of all this. He disapproved of the weekly visits with the girls to the graveside, the insistent mourning of a five-year-old for a brother she'd met only in photos. 'Why does she even need to know about him?' he demanded last week. 'Why do you have to expose her to this?'

Katherine hadn't answered. She'd carried on making notes, perfecting her lesson plan for the extra literacy class she taught at the primary school on Fridays. *Keeping my hand in,* she called it, in public. They were Year Three children, and mostly aged eight.

She hadn't said, 'Because if I don't acknowledge the fact that he's part of this family, then no one else ever will.' She knew Gus mourned privately, in silence. She sometimes stumbled across the cards he left at the grave. *For Alfie, with all my love.*

They surprised her.

Gus believed in protecting the girls from the tragedy of their older brother. But it was easier for him – he spent less time with them. Katherine couldn't pretend hour after hour, day in, day out. Pure happiness – the sort she remembered feeling just after she'd had Alfie – was out of reach for her now, and always would be. Whenever she looked at the girls, she thought of the boy who should be there beside them, and it would go on like that now, forever. There'd be a missing young man. A missing adult. Missing grandchildren. She would never be able to give her children a mother who didn't grieve.

That was why, to Gus's disgust, she involved them in Alfie's memory. But was it fair? She didn't know. He called it unnecessary pain. She called it teaching them the truth about death. They had a brother. They deserved to know about him, and he didn't deserve to be forgotten.

•

Gus was there when they got home, coming down the kitchen stairs, his arms laden with sheets stripped from the spare-room bed. No doubt he was preparing for Leila's arrival, making sure everything was perfect for her. He didn't trust Katherine to do it, and she didn't blame him. She would put no love in that particular drudgery. Leila would crawl in among sheets she'd filled with resentment. They'd give her more nightmares.

'You're home early,' she remarked.

'There were no appointments this afternoon.'

She wheeled Lily into the hallway and shut the door. She'd fallen asleep on the way home, and Katherine wanted her to stay that way for at least the next two hours. Waking her and carrying her up to her cot could prove disastrous. Not yet two years old, her youngest daughter didn't like to miss anything.

Grace was tugging at her skirt. 'Can I watch TV?'

'Yes. But don't wake your sister up.'

Quietly, Grace lifted the latch on the hall door and tiptoed away to the front room.

Gus loaded the sheets into the washing machine. 'She watches too much television.'

'Go and play with her, then,' Katherine said mildly.

He glanced back over his shoulder, scornful but wordless.

She said, 'Where are we putting Leila and Olivia when they get here?'

He pressed the start button on the washing machine, then stood up and faced her. 'Olivia can go in the spare room. Leila can go in the single room above the study.'

'So you're not putting them together?'

He frowned. 'Do you think that would be best?'

'I don't know. She's your daughter.'

'Yes. Yes, you're right. She is. But she hasn't lived with me for the last God-knows-how-long, Katherine, so I'm not entirely sure what to do with her.'

Katherine lifted the kettle and carried it to the sink. Without looking at him she said, 'Do you want some tea?'

'I'll make it. You shouldn't be doing that.'

'It's all right, Gus. It's just a kettle.'

She filled it with water, took it back to the worktop and switched it on. She turned round to face him again. 'I don't know what we should do with them. Does Leila know we know?'

He shook his head. 'I don't think so.'

'Then to begin with, we might as well pretend we don't.'

'Right.'

They were silent while the kettle boiled.

He said, 'She's very nice.'

'Who?'

'Olivia.'

'Good.'

She made the tea, carried hers to the table and sat down.

He stood with his back against the worktop and spoke slowly. 'I'm not sure whether the school got it right. I'm not sure – exactly – what's going on. They seem like good friends.'

'But with an obsessive relationship.'

'Isn't that common among girls?'

'Younger girls than Leila, I would have thought.'

'So you think she's gay?'

Katherine laughed. 'I have no idea. She might be.'

She didn't care, one way or the other, whether Leila was gay or not. She just didn't want her near her children. That was why she'd suggested a friend came home with her – to keep her attention away from the new baby when he was born. Gus had been pleased. He'd taken it as evidence that she was making an effort.

He sipped his tea. 'Strange,' was his only comment.

She assumed he was referring to his daughter's sexuality. Seventeen-year-old Leila and her lesbian lover. Privately, when she was being objective about it, Katherine found it slightly amusing. She admired the girls' pluck, their refusal to obey a clearly unliberated housemistress.

She rested her mug against her belly. The baby squirmed in response. None of the other three had been so alert. She deluded herself into believing it meant this one would be extra-sensitive, humble, caring. She stroked her hand over him. They had only three weeks to go, and there would be a boy in the house again. They were desperate for a boy. They'd resorted to experimenting with myths, having sex on the day of the month that a book had told them was most likely to result in a male child. Both their libidos had soared at the thought of creating a boy. They'd had sex three times that day – once in the morning before six, once during Lily's afternoon sleep, and then again at night. They'd hardly done it since, though, or very much before.

Gus pulled a chair out from under the table and sat down. 'I think Olivia will stay until September.'

'That's fine.' She wondered what the girl's parents were thinking of. She was only eighteen.

'They won't be in the way. They'll do their own thing. Actually, I might buy Leila a car before she gets here. I'll take her out and teach her to drive.'

'And Rosie? Will she be coming over all the time?'

He looked away from her. 'I don't know about that.'

'She'd better not be, Gus.'

She could hear the old frenzy rising in her voice again – the frenzy that, before, people had taken to mean she'd lost her mind. Not enough evidence, they said. Cot death. Accidental suffocation, not murder. But still they sympathised. They sympathised with the loss, and the depths it plunged her to. Grief of this magnitude … Well, it can cause people to lose their grip on reality for a while.

But she knew. Her grip on reality had never been lost, not for one moment. There were times when she'd wanted it to be. She'd longed to hold him, change him, feel him feeding from a body that would not accept his death and kept on and on producing milk. She'd have welcomed madness, if madness could have fooled her.

But she always knew. She always knew he was gone. And she knew – she knew with utter, deep-soul certainty – that Leila and Rosie had killed him. And she knew that Gus knew it, too. It was why he'd sent her away. To protect her.

•

After it happened, when her suspicions were strong but before she approached the police, she'd gone next door and spoken to Alison, Rosie's mother. That was her first mistake. She wondered now what had possessed her to do it, and could only put it down to the frailty of a mind overloaded. In that sense, she really had lost her grip on the world. Her thoughts had been relentless and uncontrollable, attacking her from all sides: how had her baby died, when they'd done everything they possibly could to keep him alive? Why hadn't she woken up and heard him? Why didn't some sixth sense alert her to the fact that he'd stopped breathing? Did that lack of intuition mean she was missing something vital, something other mothers had? And why was it that her baby had died, and not someone else's? Surely the enormity of her love alone had been enough to keep him alive? And couldn't her tears, now that he was gone, be powerful enough to bring him home?

The questions were endless, sometimes rational and sometimes not. They consumed her, but never was there a single answer. Except, eventually, at the inquest seven months later: suffocation by accident, because of a toy elephant in his moses basket that she knew she'd never put there.

Her second mistake, the day she'd gone to see Rosie's mother, had been in not planning what she was going to say. Until then, Alison had been staunchly compassionate and supportive, unlike most of the villagers, who'd recoiled at the sight of emotion as raw as hers, and *raw* was exactly what it was. She no longer felt wrapped in skin. She felt she was nothing but flesh – exposed, bright red and bleeding.

Those who didn't recoil offered well-meaning but badly thought out words of comfort:

'You can have another one.'

'Time will heal you.'

'At least he died young, before you got to know him. It would have been worse if he were older.'

People's comments astounded her. Time, she knew, would never heal this one. It might make it slightly easier to bear, but it would never heal. Time would go on and on – as was its habit – but she would always be without her child, missing out on every part of his life. And how, she wanted to ask, would it have been worse to lose him later? It was true that she'd had barely a past with her baby, which she knew was what they meant, but she had lost his entire future – the one that she'd indulged in daydreams about during the thirty-seven days she'd had him, adoring his newborn self, but still longing to meet him aged four, aged seven, aged eighteen.

Alison, probably because of her own losses – failure to conceive, miscarriages, years of childlessness before being offered Rosie – came closer to understanding. Six weeks after his death Katherine went round there and talked ceaselessly. She knew she'd been incoherent at times. She'd repeated things as she tried to make sense of them. She'd needed breaks for heavy weeping. And then she said, 'But I just can't believe it was an accident.'

Alison gazed at her sympathetically. Katherine hadn't told her that there were three days after the post-mortem when she'd been questioned as though she'd killed him. The police had come to the house and presented the pathologist's findings: bruising around the nose and mouth, indicative of suffocation through smothering. She'd grown ferocious with anger. Was it not enough to have lost her baby, without this? They could speak to anyone – doctors, health visitors, neighbours – and they'd all say she took proper care of him.

But the police had doubted. For three days, it had been a possible murder enquiry. And Katherine doubted, too, but not herself. Never herself.

Alison said, 'What do you mean, Katherine?'

'I mean, I don't believe it was an accident. I did everything anyone could do…'

'I know. Of course you did. But sometimes…'

Katherine faced her squarely. 'I don't believe it was an accident. I believe someone killed him.'

Shock made Alison silent.

Katherine said, 'I think it was Leila.'

'No.' Alison shook her head. 'No. Listen, listen. You're grieving. You want someone to blame. But Leila's a child. She's nine years old. And besides, Rosie was staying that night. She couldn't possibly…'

'She could. They both could.'

She watched Alison shut down her sympathy, and grow angry and defended. 'I'm sorry, but this is absurd. I can't have this conversation with you.'

'I'm not suggesting that Rosie was involved...'

'I should think not.'

'They might not have done it on purpose. But Rosie said to the police...'

'Rosie was honest. That was all. I feel for you, Katherine, I really do, but you cannot be in my house and make these accusations against my daughter. Please leave.'

So she'd left. Later, Rosie's mother became the main force in convincing the police that Katherine had lost her mind. They interviewed the girls, but they barely took her seriously. It was accidental suffocation, to everyone but Katherine. And Gus.

•

She always woke before six, to snatch an hour before the day started. Last night, Grace had crept into their bed and was still there, curled up between them, her hands resting on the round curve of Katherine's belly. Getting up would risk waking her, and this was one time Katherine hated to sacrifice – the solitary peace of the early morning. It meant more to her than sleep.

Behind the curtains, the sun had come up, but the sky was still fish grey. Gus slept on. He'd be driving to Eastbourne in a couple of hours, to pick up Leila and bring her home. She turned her head to the side and stared at him, the hulk of body in her bed. She didn't hate him. She wasn't sure, now, that she had feelings strong enough for that. The most she could summon was resentment, or contempt, but even those were dim and intermittent, and interspersed with periods of tenderness. But she felt, and had felt for some time, that his presence tarnished her life. If he weren't here, then everything she was made of would be pure: the purest love, overshadowed by the purest sorrow.

Except that it wouldn't be, of course, because if he weren't here there would be no money. She wouldn't be able to devote herself to the children and enjoy them. She'd have to go out, earn, become stressed and short-tempered, and then the children – no longer her luxuries – would constantly frustrate her. She'd seen that happen to friends who stopped spending their lives at home to face the essentials of providing.

Their lives grew out of synch with their children's. They craved even more time away.

For a year or so now, she'd resigned herself to staying with him. Besides the children and the money, he was the one person in the world who shared her loss. They hardly spoke about it, but they were the only people who could ever understand. They trapped one another. They both knew that.

But things were changing now. He was bringing Leila home.

Through the monitor beside the bed, she could hear Lily's occasional whimpers as she slept. The baby still inside her wriggled and kicked, but Grace continued to cup her hands around him. She was protective of this brother, even in sleep.

Katherine knew she had to stay calm, but her instinct was growing stronger and her instinct was to pack up the children and leave. She gazed upwards at the ceiling. It was his house. He wasn't going to move out. He'd lived here since before Leila was born. He'd lived here with his wife. There'd been a time, when Katherine first met him, when he'd wanted to sell it. He'd changed his mind, of course. Because of Leila. Because Leila, aged eight, had seemed so deeply troubled.

Grace rolled over suddenly and kicked him in her sleep. He snorted and moved, then woke. 'What time is it?'

'Long before seven. Don't worry.'

Slowly, he slid his arms under Grace's body, lifted her up and carried her back to her room. She didn't wake.

Katherine heard him go downstairs. He banged cupboards and cutlery in the kitchen. When he came back, he brought two cups of tea. He passed one to her. This was what Saturday mornings in bed involved now: drinking tea together in silence.

He surprised her. He didn't look at her, but he said, 'You know I'd never bring her home if I thought it was going to hurt our family.'

For a while, she said nothing. Finally, he looked at her again. 'You must know that.'

She raised a hand to her mouth. He reached out and pulled it away.

This was the closest he'd ever come to mentioning Leila's capacity to hurt them. Most of the time, he idolised her.

'Yes.' She nodded. 'I do know.'

Because despite everything, she did know. She knew Grace and Lily meant just as much to him as Leila did. But there was desperation in his love for Leila – a desperate need to believe in her.

He sighed, relieved, and then he kissed her.

•

They hadn't wanted a boy to replace Alfie. They'd wanted the experience of a son again. Katherine tried explaining this to her mother, who disapproved of designer babies believed the sex of every child should be a surprise at birth. Essentially, Katherine agreed with her. But losing Alfie had opened a new, huge need in her – the need to care for a boy until he reached adulthood. She was unfinished. She was unfinished as the mother of a son.

She glanced at the grandfather clock in the corner of the room. Gus had left nearly three hours ago. She was restless and anxious waiting for them to arrive, and too heavily pregnant now to do anything. Outside was hot, too hot. She longed for rain to bring relief, for clouds to shut out the glare of the sun.

She sat with her hands cradled round her middle. She would protect this baby. She would not let this one die. She wasn't going to allow Leila to come anywhere near him, no matter what Gus said.

He'd talked to her about it this morning in bed, for the first time – carefully and with guarded words. But it was a start.

'I know what you think,' he said. 'I know you still think it had something to do with Leila.'

Until recently, she'd have denied that with silence. She'd have done anything she could to avoid the argument. The argument was bottomless. There was no way to resolve it. It would break them.

Instead, this time, she said, 'What do you think?'

He sighed heavily. 'I think…' He stopped and shook his head. 'I understand…' Finally, he shrugged. 'I don't know.'

The admission was huge and helpless.

He was silent for a while before he spoke again. 'I know what led you to those conclusions. I do understand. But she was so young. She was a child. She didn't know what she was doing.'

'So you think she did it?'

'The coroner at the inquest didn't think so. That's the one thing I have.'

'The coroner at the inquest was told by several people that I was mad.' She paused. 'Alfie didn't just die in his sleep, Gus. He was suffocated. I – *we* – would never have let that happen. The coroner knew that, the police knew that…'

'I know all this.'

'But you think he just suffocated in his sleep, just like that? After all the care we'd ever taken?'

'I don't know.' He was quiet then for a long time. 'But what I do know is that if it did involve Leila, if it really did, then it's not because she was an evil child. She was confused. She would never have deliberately…' He shook his head. Even now, disbelief had the power to hinder his words.

'OK.' She shrugged. 'Maybe that's true.'

'You don't agree.'

She didn't answer. The fact was, she didn't care.

He carried on. 'And whatever happened, whatever there is we don't know about, she isn't that child anymore. She'll be eighteen in December. She's intelligent, she works hard, she's an adult now, for goodness' sake. She's not the person she was when she was nine.'

He raised his head and looked at her. She looked away. He stood up, went to the wardrobe, got dressed. The conversation was finished.

•

She heard his car pulling into the driveway. She picked up Lily from the floor and sat her on the worktop. Immediately, Lily reached for a whisk and a wooden spoon from the utensils pot on the side and started banging the surface. Katherine let her.

She leaned forwards and peered out through the window at the side. She could see the red sheen of Gus's car between the gaps in the trees. A door opened and a tall female body stepped out. Her hair was long – contained in a single plait, blonde, thick as rope.

II

Olivia

Some weeks ago, spring had erupted into summer, and now suddenly the world outside was vivid and intense, as though some slowly rotating dial on the side of the earth had been turned too far, and brought too much colour. The ocean and the sky, which in winter had merely been dismal grey backdrops, came forwards, brilliant blue and invasive. The sun dazzled the cliff faces, and even the cliff top roads became blacker as they warmed and began to soften.

All this felt sudden, though perhaps it hadn't been. For weeks and weeks, we'd been so busy with exams, the seasons were passing us by. Everyone had shut themselves in their rooms, vaguely aware that the air outside was bright. The sixth form boarding house at Rotherfield was old and dim, no doubt a deliberate manoeuvre on the part of the headmistress. She shoved us all away in the darkest part of the school, steadfastly believing that lack of exposure to sunlight would discourage our desires to go outside, promote good study habits, and miraculously result in the country's top exam grades.

Gus picked us up and drove us back to Ash Farm on the hottest day of the year so far. I sat in the back of the car, watching in the rear view mirror as Rotherfield Hall slipped further and further behind us. I didn't feel sad to be leaving, but I couldn't help thinking of our empty rooms, and imagining who'd be in them next year, living among all our memories. The memories still felt tangible to me, and I wondered whether the new girls would sense them, or see them there. Yesterday, we'd carved our names into the headboards of all the beds we'd ever slept in together. Leila and Olivia. I wasn't sure why we'd done it. Perhaps we were marking territory. Perhaps it was a pseudo-poetic shot at immortality. (Leila liked the way each name held the echo of the other.) Either way, we were there forever now, for everyone to see.

We drove deeper into Kent. The towns and all their concrete faded away, and there were only fields and forests unfolding ahead of us for miles. I picked up my bag from the seat beside me and checked inside it. I'd bought wine and chocolates for Gus and Katherine, and a present for each of the girls and the new baby. Leila said I didn't need to do that, but I wanted the atmosphere when we arrived to be friendly. Although I didn't expect to like Katherine, it was important for her to like me. I didn't want her to send me home.

•

Ash Farm was bigger than I'd imagined. They said it was the oldest building in the village after the church, and it was set in grounds full of copper beech trees and silver birches that shone lightly in the breeze. Countless bushes at the front of the garden were slung with red and white roses. Bees hovered among them, knocking their petals to the ground. At the side of the house stood a barn, and a coop full of chickens scratching at the dry cracked earth. The only sounds here were small: the creaking of wood in the trees; water; the rumble of a distant plane.

They owned a lot of land. Beyond the garden was a paddock, which backed onto the river. A family of peacocks lived there. Leila said they'd been a present from her father to Katherine several years ago. They dropped their feathers, and the children often brought them into the house, which alarmed Katherine, as it threatened bad luck. They'd had enough of that, she said, and no one was taking any more chances. *Grabbing at straws,* I thought, but then, I'd never experienced tragedy, and could see how people might clutch at anything to stop it from happening again.

We followed Gus through a side door that led to the kitchen. The kitchen was ancient, and also beautiful. The whole ceiling was crossed with beams. They were full of tiny holes, put there by either time or woodworm. A black Aga burned at one end, and a wooden table stretched almost the full length of the room. In the corner was a wooden ladder, leading upwards to a trap door. The trap door was open, but all I could see beyond it were floorboards.

A woman stood at the table with her back towards us, chopping salad and tossing it into a wooden bowl. And there was a baby, sitting on the edge of the worktop, chewing the handle of a wooden spoon.

Gus set Leila's suitcase down on the floor. He said, 'We're here.'

The woman turned around. She moved slowly, heavy with the weight of her pregnancy. Her hair was brown, and swept into a silver clip behind her head. A few strands had escaped and dangled about her face. Her features were soft. I'd expected her to be harder, and more careworn, but she was very, very pretty. She smiled warmly, but before she spoke she lifted the baby from the worktop and held her against the side of her body. She held out a hand for me to shake. 'Hello, Olivia,' she said. 'I'm glad you could come.'

I smiled, and thought, *So this is Katherine. This is the woman who has caused so much of Leila's grief.*

The normality of her appearance surprised me, and then kept on surprising me.

She stood in front of us and stroked the baby's hair. 'This is Lily,' she said. 'She's nearly two.' The pride in her voice was unmistakable. Lily buried her face in her mother's shoulder. Katherine continued, 'Leila can show you to your room, I'm sure.' Then for the first time, the two of them looked at each other.

'Hello, Leila.' Her voice became cold.

Leila dropped her gaze. 'Hello.'

Lily squirmed in Katherine's arms, wanting to be put down, but Katherine continued to hold her. She said, 'You're sleeping in the single room above the study, is that OK?'

Leila nodded.

'And Olivia's in the room at the front, overlooking the garden. It's the only spare one we have now the girls both sleep on their own, unless you want to go back up to the attic, Leila. There's still your old bed up there.'

'No, thanks. It's fine. I'll stay downstairs.'

She picked up her suitcase. I did the same, ready to follow her.

Katherine looked at Gus. 'Grace is upstairs. She's in her room.'

He turned away. 'Right.'

'Are you going to go up with the girls?'

'No. They can manage. Leila knows the way.' He turned round to us again, and ruffled Leila's hair.

I followed her through the kitchen to the hall, and then into another room full of beams and exposed bricks. An inglenook fireplace completely owned one wall. Above it on the mantelpiece burned an ivory church candle. I wondered why, as it gave no light. I found out later that it was a memorial, flaming perpetually.

The room smelled of logs and old damp. Leila unlatched the door in the far corner and we creaked up the stairs to the landing. Another little girl stood in the shadow of a doorway. She watched us.

Leila said, 'Hello, Grace.'

Grace stayed silent.

Leila knelt down on the floor in front of her. She put out her hand. 'Can I see what you've got?'

Slowly, Grace held out a small wooden doll. Then, without warning, she snatched it back again. 'I'm not supposed to talk to you unless my mum's here.'

Leila stood up. She put her hand on my arm. 'It's this way,' she said.

I followed her round a corner to my room. There was a four-poster bed, and beside it on the floor an old wicker basket full of blankets and soft toys.

I put my suitcase down and sat on the bed. 'Are you all right?' I asked.

'I'm fine,' she said. She opened the window and looked out over the garden.

'Why won't she let Grace talk to you?'

Her laugh was brittle. 'Because she's mad.'

I said nothing. I was confused, and wondered whether I should have come.

•

The day passed slowly. Once, at lunchtime, they mentioned Alfie. I hadn't expected that. I'd expected him to be a secret, something painful and uncomfortable that no one could bring themselves to refer to.

It was Grace who spoke. We were eating lunch on the terrace by the swimming pool, which they'd dug in the years since Leila had been away. Politely, Katherine asked me about my family. I said, 'My parents live in America. I have a brother I never see.'

Grace said, 'I never see my brother, either. He died before I was born. He was just a baby then, but now he's eight.'

The silence that fell was excruciating. The heat of the day was at its most intense. The gazebo we sat under was thatched, and attracted insects. Flies droned over our food. Gus slapped one away with the back of his hand. Leila, sitting next to me, hunched her shoulders and bent over her plate and didn't eat.

Only Katherine spoke. 'Not now, Grace.'

I glanced at her. She was looking straight at Leila and me, and for a moment, our eyes met. Fleetingly, an expression of pain crossed her face, and then she turned her attention to Lily, sitting in the highchair beside her. I tried to imagine her life, and couldn't.

It was the only time he was mentioned that day, but he was everywhere.

•

At night, we went to bed early. I was waiting for Leila to come to my room. I stood at the window and closed the curtains. The shriek of peacocks drifted in from outside. It still wasn't completely dark, despite there being no moon.

I thought of the sorrow this house had seen and it made me shudder. I wondered why they hadn't moved, and started again. Leila said it was because they couldn't. Six years went by before they'd even cleared out the nursery.

I started unpacking and found a photo of us, and stood it on the bedside table. It had been taken at school, before they moved us out of the room we shared. Remembering it made me oddly homesick, as though everything we'd had between us had been left behind that morning.

I kicked my empty suitcase under the bed. I heard it knock against something hard, which cracked. I bent down and looked. Underneath my case was an old white plaster cast, broken in two. I pulled the pieces out and slotted them together. They formed a shape like a frame containing two baby footprints. Underneath, someone had etched the year, and then

Alfie

February 15th – March 24th

I held it in my hands and stared at it. It made my stomach sway. I'd always known about him, for almost as long as I'd known Leila, but this was the only thing I'd ever seen, and for the first time I thought, *He was real, and he died.*

The door behind me opened. Quickly, I pushed the cast back under the bed.

Leila came in, draped in her white dressing gown. She said, 'You aren't in bed yet.'

She turned on the lamps and switched off the overhead light. I started to undress. On the wall above the fireplace were framed photographs of babies. I stood for a moment and looked at them.

Leila said, 'They're all Alfie.'

I picked out a photo of a blonde-haired child, holding him close to her chest. I said, 'Is that you?'

'Yes. It's the day before he died.' Casually, she said, 'This is his room, you know.'

'Sorry?'

'This.' She gestured expansively. 'It's his bedroom.'

The present tense surprised me, but I was beginning to realise that time didn't move forwards here. It just spun round and round, circling an old date, endlessly.

III

Leila

My mother had gone. Obediently, as all problems were supposed to, she went when I told someone about her. After I'd spoken to Rosie that night I stayed at her house, the nightmares decreased and then stopped. Everybody thought I was better. They thought the herald of a new family was doing me good. My father stopped sending me to the woman after school. Possibly, that that was a mistake on his part. But possibly not. No one will ever know what might never have happened if they'd left me there, to talk about my mother and dead sibling in a room full of cruelly-abused dolls. Perhaps it would have healed me. Perhaps I'd have renewed my old interests in making daisy chains and solving word search puzzles.

Katherine went into labour in the middle of the night. I heard her wailing from my room in the attic. She swore a lot. She was having the baby at home. I never understood why. My father abandoned her between contractions to take me round to Rosie's house. Outside, it had been snowing for the first time in years. The fields and the trees glowed white through the dark. The day before, Rosie told me that some women died when they gave birth. A world of white light seemed an appropriate farewell. A brief descent by heaven to earth.

My father left after Alison let me in. Rosie was in bed. I hadn't got dressed to go over there and still wore my pyjamas. Alison gave me a mug of warm milk from the stove. She said we had a long wait ahead of us, and I should go to Rosie's room and get some sleep. I didn't want to. I didn't want to spend all this time with Rosie. Rosie was into assertiveness. She said I didn't have enough of it. She'd decided to test me by being vicious and cruel. If I stood up for myself, I scored points. If not, I was stupid. But it was impossible to know when she was testing and when she was just being herself. If I became assertive at the wrong times, Rosie was even worse.

I did go to her room as her mother told me. I edged myself into her bed slowly, so I wouldn't wake her up. The springs creaked. Rosie mumbled something, but I couldn't tell what it was. Her sleep breath came in and out and I could feel it against my face. It smelled sour.

•

When we woke, the baby hadn't been born. Rosie and I stayed in her room all morning, waiting. It was half-term, and the day stretched out before us, desolate except for our certainty of Katherine's pain, and the promise of a child at the end of it.

We hated her by then, Rosie and me. I hated her because she wasn't my mother. Rosie hated her because Rosie hated everyone, or at least, she hated everyone normal. I realised later, after I'd met Olivia, that what she couldn't bear was to see other people's happiness. It was crucial to her to destroy it. And she never changed. Even at twenty, she was just the same.

She stood on a stool and rummaged around on the shelf at the top of her wardrobe. She brought down an old carrier bag. 'Look,' she said. She took out an old scrapbook and a packet of cigarettes. She held the cigarettes out in front of me. 'Have you ever had one?'

'No.'

'I've had these ever since I was in the children's home. I stole them from one of the other girls there. She was fifteen. She went mad when she found out they'd gone.'

She took one out of the packet and held it between her fingers. 'You can have one if you like, but not here. We'll have to go outside.' She glanced towards the door. 'No one knows I've got them. I hid them when I moved out the kids' home. I hid them in a box of tissues.' She laughed. 'Did you know they kill you?'

'Yes.'

'Do you want one?'

'OK.'

'First you have to look at this,' she said, and opened the scrapbook. It was full of photos. 'That's my real mum.'

I looked. The woman in the picture was sitting in a chair, smoking. Her hair was white-blonde and stiff and spiky. She didn't look like anyone's mother.

Rosie turned the page. 'That's my sister.'

The girl looked about ten. She, too, had a cigarette in her hand. Clearly, Rosie's family were determined to face death young, head-on.

I said, 'Where does she live now?'

Rosie shrugged. 'She had a baby when she was fourteen. She lives up north. I never see her.' She paused. 'I've got a brother as well, but the social workers took him away when he was born. I was in the kids' home then, so I never saw him.'

These were new ideas to me. I'd never heard of children having children, or babies being taken at birth. I asked, 'Why did they take him?'

Rosie rolled her eyes. 'Because my mum was a hooker and a drug addict.'

'Oh.'

'She hated kids. She hated babies. Everyone hates babies eventually. They think they're going to be sweet, but once they come along, they realise. They realise then how bad they are.' She looked at me sideways. 'You'll realise that, too. And Katherine will.'

I thought about it for a while, and I remembered the letter I'd found in the cellar. It was from my mother to her friends in Australia. They'd sent it back to my father after she died. It was all about me when I was a baby, and her plans to have more. I said, 'But my mum didn't hate them. She loved them. She wanted four.'

Rosie's words were sharp and abrupt. 'Your mother's dead. She hasn't got any kids at all.'

Downstairs, the phone rang. Rosie jumped up. 'I bet that's your dad. Wait there.'

I wondered whether this might be one of those times I was intended to assert myself. I said, 'I'll come with you.'

Rosie stood against the door, her arms and legs splayed so I couldn't leave.

'No. I said wait here. I'll find out what's going on. Then I'll come back and tell you.'

While she was gone, I knelt on the bed and stared at the snow outside. I was nine by then. My birthday was the 21st December. My father told me that, despite being the darkest day of the year, it was a day to be celebrated, as it meant the return of the sun. But I'd always longed for snow on my birthday. Despite everything, I still wanted magic, and the world had looked magic that day, just before Alfie was born.

The bedroom door opened again and Rosie came back in. She stood in front of me, and bent her head down low.

I turned round. 'Was that my dad?'

Rosie nodded.

'What did he say?'

She stayed quiet before she spoke. Then she said. 'It's taking a really long time. Things are going wrong.'

'What things?'

'Everything. Pretty much.'

'Can I go home?'

'Of course you can't go home. Katherine's there, screaming her head off.'

'Is my dad OK?'

'Of course. *He*'s fine. It's Katherine and the baby who might not be. And I know why.'

'Why?'

'It's your mother.'

'What do you mean?'

'It is. You said yourself she wanted children. You said yourself she used to visit you. Now she wants to kill Katherine. She wants that baby for herself.'

I knew this was another game. I knew the phone call probably hadn't been my father. But I didn't know what to say, so I just said, 'Liar.'

Rosie shrugged. 'You'll see, Leila,' she said. 'You'll see.'

•

In the afternoon, Rosie dragged me through the village on her sledge. She stopped at the entrance to the churchyard. 'You need to get off here.'

I looked up at the church. 'Why?'

'Because we're going to visit your mother.'

'I don't want to.'

'It doesn't matter whether you want to or not. You have to. Come on.'

She took my hand and led me to the garden. Beneath the trees along the footpath, the snow was muddy and wet. I slipped, but didn't fall. We moved further down the path and I could see the garden between the gaps in the trees, buried under snow that stretched for miles. I shivered. I thought how cold it must be under the earth by now. My mind drifted to my doll, in her grave among the fir trees.

I said, 'Why do we have to come here?'

For a while, she didn't answer. I followed her into the garden at the end of the path, and saw different sets of footprints that had made tracks in the snow towards the gravestones. Rosie looked at her watch. She said, 'You have to ask your mother to stop haunting Katherine.'

The easiest thing to do when Rosie was like this was to agree. I wanted her to like me. More than anything, I wanted her approval. Her approval was hard to win, and all the sweeter for that when it came. But I didn't want to do this today. I said, 'I don't think she is haunting her.'

'Of course she is. Why else would everything be going wrong? Your dad told my mum Katherine might be dying. Things like this don't happen all the time. It must be your mother. She's dead and she's really angry.'

I hesitated. Then I said, 'But maybe she should be angry. Maybe she's angry with Katherine for trying to get rid of me.' I knew, by then, that Katherine had stopped trying. Now, she and I were competing. A grown woman and a little girl. We were competing for my father's love, and she was winning.

Rosie raised her eyebrows. 'I don't think that's a good enough reason to try and kill her, do you?'

I shrugged.

We walked over to my mother's grave. There were a few snowflakes gathered at the top of the headstone. I touched one with my fingertip. It melted.

Rosie lowered her voice. 'You have to kneel down.'

I looked at the ground. 'No, I don't.'

'You do. Go on.'

She waited.

I stood beside the grave and did nothing.

'Go on,' Rosie said again. 'Kneel down.'

I knelt in the snow.

'Now you have to clasp your hands together like this.' She held out her hands to show me. 'And you have to bow your head like this, and you have to ask your mother to leave them alone, and to make Katherine well, and to make sure the baby is born soon and not to hurt it.'

I started murmuring some words, but they were quiet, because I didn't want her to hear them.

She stood above me. 'I can't hear you,' she said. 'You'll have to speak louder. If I can't hear you, there's no way your mother will be able to.'

I spoke louder. When I'd finished, I stood up again. The bottoms of my jeans were wet with snow. Rosie put her arm around me. 'You don't need to feel bad. It's not your fault.'

We started walking away. Rosie kept her arm around my shoulders.

•

She had her cigarettes and a rusty lighter in her coat pocket. On the way home, she ducked suddenly behind an oak tree and lit one. 'Here.' She handed another one out to me. 'Try it.'

I took it and held it in my fingers. My father hated smoking. He was a doctor. He'd diagnosed hundreds of cases of lung cancer. It struck me how good a cigarette must be, if people were willing to die for another one. It looked quite innocent there in my hands – long and white, with thin joined-up writing curling around the end beneath the filter. I put it in my mouth. Rosie leant forwards with the lighter.

I choked, of course. I choked out long swirls of blue smoke. Rosie smirked, but left it at that. She didn't force me to finish. She just stood with her back against the tree, and smoked her own cigarette to the tip.

•

By the time we got back to Rosie's house, stinking of smoke and nicotine, Alfie had been born. Alison walked me home. I knew Rosie was watching from her window as I trudged over the snow to meet the latest addition to my re-formed family. Rosie's resentment travelled. It was tangible. It shone. It surrounded her like a halo.

Up in the bedroom, the baby was lying in Katherine's arms, curled up in a blanket. I bent over and peered at him. His mouth moved, as though he were sucking on air. My father stood back and watched, delighted.

Katherine's face looked pale against the pillows. She didn't say very much. She just smiled. I found out afterwards that she was euphoric, and hadn't spoken for fear of sounding insane. She'd also wanted to be alone with her baby. Her world had shrunk. There was no room for anyone else.

I reached out and touched the spike of Alfie's hair. It was damp. Katherine passed him to me. His head lolled, but his eyes stayed closed. As I held him, he began to cry. Even the crying was feeble. Katherine wanted him back then, and I laughed, and smelled the smoke on my breath. His smallness and vulnerability should have suffused me with feminine devotion. They didn't. I'd met someone, at last, weaker and more helpless than I was.

•

I'd never been a violent child. I'd never pulled wings and legs off insects, or felt awe at the bloody entrails of a cat's or a fox's kill. That was the business of other children, although not Rosie, of course. She was one step ahead. She had no time for the baser forms of life. Her concern was with human misery.

Once, only once until that time, had I inflicted pain on something that wasn't me. In the spring when I was eight, before Rosie had moved in next door, and when my father still worked every hour he had to fill, I stepped by accident on the foot of a duckling. It squealed and squealed, but I didn't move. I waited, and watched it, flailing beneath my sandal, and then I twisted my heel hard against its rubbery webbed foot. It squealed again, and somewhere inside me, I felt release at that expression of pain, and I let go. It couldn't walk. A few days later, I found it lying dead at the roadside, fluffy and yellow, with one mangled foot, and I thought, *I did that.* I was mortified. I grieved. I was also darkly triumphant.

Four or five years afterwards, as we entered our teens at Rotherfield Hall, it was self-loathing that became the blood sport. Girls gagged on their own fingers, or hacked at their arms with knives. They starved themselves skeletal. I understood. I knew the relief that came with puke or pain, the cleansing gratification of blood on skin. I did it myself, in the days before Olivia came. Punishment. A temporary retribution on my spirit. Oh, I would stay relentlessly unhealed.

I understood Rosie then, and her addiction to cruelty. Torture was torture. You didn't need to feel it yourself to gain its benefits.

She came over with her mother when Alfie was one week old. Upstairs in my attic room, she asked me, 'Do you like having a baby in your house?'

I said, 'It's OK. He cries a lot in the night, though, and wakes everyone up. That's a bit annoying.'

'Does Katherine like him?'

'I suppose so. She must.'

'Can we go down and look at him?'

'I'm not supposed to go near him when he's asleep, in case I wake him up.'

'Come on. We'll be quiet,' Rosie said, and she walked over to the top of the stairs.

I followed her down the steps to the landing. I crept across the floor to my father's room, where the door was still slightly open, and I paused with my ear against the wood to make sure Katherine had definitely gone. The sounds of lullaby music came snaking out towards me, from the mobile above Alfie's basket.

I looked up and whispered, 'She's gone. It's OK. But be really quiet.'

I pushed open the door.

The room now was full of Alfie's things. Babygros and miniature cardigans lay on every surface, along with piles of nappies, cotton wool, blankets and little toys. The baby monitor stood on the windowsill. It had a ring of lights at the top that flashed green when the baby was silent and red when he cried.

Rosie tiptoed over to the baby. She stood above his bed and looked down at him. Then she whispered, 'Do you think he looks like Katherine?'

I pointed to the monitor. 'We need to be really quick.'

'OK.'

Alfie sighed. Rosie bent over him and brushed his hair with her fingers. Then she faced me with one hand on her hip. 'When he came home, did they cut some of his hair off?'

'I don't know. I don't think so.'

Rosie shook her head. 'Well, they were supposed to. You should always cut off a lock of a newborn baby's hair. Otherwise it's bad luck.'

I wasn't sure whether to believe her. But I remembered the lock of my own hair in the cellar.

Rosie said, 'Have you got any scissors? Let's do it now.'

I hesitated.

'Come on. We'll have to be quick. Before Katherine comes up.'

I crossed the hall to the bathroom and took a pair of metal scissors from the medicine cabinet.

When I went back to the bedroom again, Rosie was standing over the baby. The expression on her face was odd – pensive and hard. 'Have you found them?' she asked.

'Yes.'

'Do you want to do it, or shall I?'

'You can.'

I stood beside her as she bent down and clasped a piece of the baby's hair between her fingers. She waited for a moment to see if he woke up. Then, when he stayed sleeping, she cut it away with the scissors and handed them back to me. 'There. We just need to find somewhere to keep it now.'

Downstairs, a door opened. We looked at each other, then ran away out of the room, and back upstairs to the attic.

•

The snow clung to the fields and hung in the trees for another week, then it melted and turned to floods. One day, at the beginning of March, the heating in my school broke down and we all had to stay at home. My father had gone back to work and Katherine was tired. Alfie cried all the time. It made them worry that he might be sick. He woke up every two hours in the night, and sometimes he cried so loudly for so long it made Katherine cry as well. I'd overheard her on the phone to her mother, saying she felt she was never going to sleep again.

Alfie was crying again now. I sat on my bed, reading. The door at the bottom of my stairs was closed, but I could still hear him, wailing and wailing and wailing. I put my book down, then crossed the room to my desk. I lifted the leg up from the floor. Beneath it was the key to my secret chest. I unlocked it and took out the tiny posy I'd made this morning, from all the smallest flowers in one of Katherine's bouquets. I'd folded the stems inside a wet piece of tissue so they wouldn't die, then wrapped some foil around them to keep them dry, and laid the posy on top of an envelope I kept Alfie's hair in.

I dropped the posy in my rucksack, along with my fairy doll, and carried it downstairs to the kitchen. Katherine and Alfie were through the hall, in the living room. I couldn't see them, but I could hear them. Katherine was talking in a low voice, and Alfie's cries were quieter now. No one had noticed his missing chunk of hair. My father said it was supposed to fall out, and Rosie had cut it underneath, closest to the skin on his head.

I went out through the back door and walked round the house to the gate at the side. It opened onto the front garden. When I reached the fir trees, I pulled back the branches and stepped inside the hollow where my other doll was buried. I often took her flowers. I had some pretend grass, as well. It was made of sheets of green plastic, and a few days ago I'd laid four of them over the grave and found stones to hold them down and make sure they didn't fly away in the wind.

I unwrapped the foil and the tissue from the posy, then knelt down and laid each flower on the grave. I wondered how cold it would be under the earth now, and whether her body might be covered with worms. The thought made me feel sick. I took the fairy doll out of my rucksack, and sat her beside the flowers. One of her wings was missing, but her hair still fell to the ground.

I waited for a while before stepping out through the trees. The sun hid behind the sky, which was grey instead of blue. In the garden, moles had built their tunnels and left earthy hills over the grass. I ran, weaving in and out of them until I reached the living room window. I was going to tap on the glass, but when I looked in I saw Katherine holding Alfie in front of her. His face was screwed up and red with anger. Katherine was crying.

Silently, I turned around and crept away, back to the side door that led to the kitchen, and upstairs to my room. I sat down on my bed and picked up the book from the table beside it. Before Alfie was born, my father had said that having a baby would make everyone happy. Sometimes it seemed to, but not always.

•

I escaped from the house and spent my time with Rosie instead. Other people who visited us cooed and fussed over Alfie. Rosie didn't. She had no interest in babies, or toddlers, or families that were neat and intact.

I went round there at the weekend. She opened the front door and she was dressed in a long black skirt and a baggy black jumper, and she had thick black lines that she'd drawn on her eyelids with a pen. Her face was pale, almost white, but her lips were red and glossy. She looked at me and said, 'Come upstairs.'

I followed her to her room. The curtains were pulled and it was dark, but the flames of two candles flickered on a table beside the bed. I faltered in the doorway.

Rosie stood in the middle of the room. 'Come on,' she said. 'Don't be scared. Sit down.'

So I sat down.

She said, 'My aunt stayed last night. She's been teaching me how to read the future. Look.' She reached behind her and took a purple silk cloth off her table and handed it to me. 'Open it,' she said.

I opened it. Inside was a pack of cards I'd never seen before. They were painted with moons and rivers and skies full of stars. There were queens and knights, and yellow goblets and gold coins and silver swords.

I said, 'They're really pretty.' I couldn't imagine what you did with them. There were no games I could think of. 'Where did you get them?'

Rosie shot an anxious glance at the door and lowered her voice, 'I stole them.'

I giggled, 'Really?'

She nodded. 'Yes. They're my aunt's. She uses them to read futures. People pay her money, but she's rubbish at it, so it doesn't matter.'

'What do you mean?'

'I mean, she told my mother she was going to have three children by the time she was thirty-five, and look: she's forty-one, she's only got me, and I'm not even hers.'

'What will your aunt say when she finds out you took them?'

Rosie shrugged. 'I don't care. She'll never find out. Anyway, I'm going to read your cards for you. Are you ready?'

'Yes.'

I held out my hands, but Rosie said, 'You have to pick the cards yourself. Pick the top four.'

I did, and I put them on the floor in a pile.

'Now spread them out on the rug.'

I spread them out, and Rosie turned them over, so their pictures were facing upwards. She studied them for a while, then nodded her head and said, 'Right. Just as I thought. This is a message from your mother.'

I felt my hands growing hot. 'What do you mean?'

Rosie lowered her voice to just above a whisper. 'Your mother has been in contact, Leila. She is very, very upset. She used to be angry, but now she's just too sad.'

I caught my breath. I knew this was another one of Rosie's games, but it was hard not to be scared.

Rosie continued. She said, 'Your mother is hurt that your dad's with

Katherine and they've got the baby. You know, she thinks the baby is hers.'

'She does not.'

'She does. Katherine is cruel, and she wants to take everything that was your mother's and make it hers. She's already got your dad and the house and you. And now she's got the baby, too. And your mother's lonely. She wants him to be with her. And she wants the other one, too. The one that you said died.'

I wished now that I'd never told Rosie about the baby in the car crash. I said, 'Well, what am I supposed to do?'

Rosie sighed. 'That's up to you. I suppose you'll just have to talk to your dad about it, or tell Katherine she has to leave him.'

'Ok.'

'You'll do it?'

'Yes.'

'Tonight?'

'Yes.'

'As soon as you get in?'

'Yes.'

'Ok. Good. Then come over tomorrow and tell me what they say.'

'OK,' I said. I knew I'd have to lie to Rosie and make everything up, because although I knew this was another one of her games, I wasn't sure how I could stop playing them.

•

In the evening, I walked home slowly. It was dark now, and I was afraid. The gravel in the driveway crunched beneath my feet. I tried to creep, so no one would know I was there. The branches on the willow by the gate shook and dropped their leaves in the wind.

The light was on in the kitchen, but no one was there when I went inside. I took off my coat and hung it on the back of a chair. I could hear the noise of the television coming from the living room.

On the table by the fruit bowl were the new photos of Alfie. My father and Katherine took photos of him all the time, even if he were only sleeping. I opened the packet and looked through them, then took one out and went upstairs to my room.

I unlocked my secret chest and put the photo inside it at the bottom, with the picture of my parents on their wedding day. I took out the photo of myself as a baby with my mother, and thought of the things Rosie had said.

I sat on the bed, and looked at the photo for a long time. Then I took a paperclip out of one of the compartments in my desk tidy and clipped it to the picture of Alfie, so the two of them could be together again.

IV

Olivia

Eastbourne was hardly a metropolis, but I'd never stayed as far into the countryside as this before. I liked it, even though it meant we couldn't go anywhere. We were used to having our freedom curbed, and at school they'd never really let us do anything – there was no way they'd have been able to explain missing daughters to parents who paid ten thousand a year to have them babysat. Occasionally, we were allowed to go to Brighton, but not very often, as they didn't want to risk exposing us to homosexuality or too much bohemia. There were also more condoms left on Brighton beach than Eastbourne, and that was not regarded as the sort of civilised behaviour we needed to be influenced by.

Gus and Katherine lived right in the heart of Kent, and the village was old – full of sixteenth-century weavers' cottages, oast houses and huge Tudor halls set back from the road. Ash Farm stood on the outskirts, on the edge of a lane that circled the village, overlooking fields and woods and an orchard. The trees were already heavy with apples. The year's heat had knocked the seasons out of place and the harvest was coming too early. The ground was desperate for water. Flowers, which a couple of weeks ago had been vivid and abundant, were beginning to wilt now in their beds of cracked earth, and the bushes had all shed their roses.

The heat and the light made it difficult to sleep. Nearly every morning, I got up early and left Leila in bed, where she would stay for hours, sleeping on and on. She'd never done this when we were at school. Days in bed back then had been luxurious and intense. Maybe she was recovering from the exhaustion of exams – she'd worked hard, hours and hours every day – but I still found it vaguely insulting that she was willing to sleep away our last two months together. It didn't occur to me that this could be the beginning of a despair that was simply going to grow now that she was back here, with the past all around her and no work to fill the spaces in her mind.

I spent my early mornings with Katherine, who usually got up when the children got up, which was sometimes around five and never later than seven. Lily had started climbing out of her cot. One morning I came downstairs while Katherine was still in bed and I found her alone in the kitchen, sitting in front of the fridge, her hands sunk into a lemon pie. Katherine, although alarmed that she hadn't heard her, found it funny. Her patience seemed to be endless. I'd never heard her lose her temper, or even raise her voice. I felt sure the world must have seen nothing like this outside Nazareth.

We'd been at Ash Farm now for around two weeks. Katherine was due to go into labour at any moment, and she looked worn out with the heat and the weight of the baby. She asked me to go out to the hen house, to hunt down eggs for the girls' breakfast, while she dealt with Lily, who had just hurled herself, screaming, to the floor and was pounding it with her fists. The floor was made of stone and it looked painful. I thought, *She'll kill herself at fifteen if she's a masochist at two*, though Katherine insisted it was normal.

I picked up a basket from the worktop and went outside. It wasn't yet eight, but already the temperature was over twenty-five. It was the longest heatwave we'd had in England for years, and also the most extreme. Much of the country had come to a halt – train tracks were melting, offices were closing, no one went out for the midday sun.

The chickens squabbled and pecked one another as I scattered grain over the ground. I rummaged through their house and found five eggs among the straw, then, just as I was heading back to the kitchen, I heard the strange sound of a girl's voice crying out.

I looked up. In the house next door, a young woman about the same age as me, or possibly a bit older, was leaning out of an upstairs window. Her hands were clutching the woodwork outside, her eyes closed and her face arranged in an expression of bliss. Behind her, a man stood naked, grasping her waist as he thrust energetically backwards and forwards.

I didn't think of myself as prudish, but the exhibitionism shocked me. I turned away, but before I did the girl opened her eyes, and for a moment our gazes locked. She stared straight at me and turned up the volume of her ecstasy.

I walked back to the house. Behind me, the couple continued. I went inside, uncomfortable and guilty. The moment I'd just shared with that stranger had been intimate and, for her, erotic, and I felt peculiarly as though I'd just betrayed Leila.

•

I found out later that the girl at the window was Rosie. Leila had mentioned her before, and for some reason, I didn't tell her now about my first liaison with her childhood tormenter. I was hoping she'd disappear.

She didn't. That afternoon, we were lying outside by the pool, and she came over, squeezing herself between the bars of the fence that separated the farthest end of her garden from Leila's. She wore a black bikini, the bottoms of which were held together at the side with two gold metal clasps. They looked precarious. She adjusted them as she sat down.

'Do you mind if I join you?' she asked. 'I was sitting on my own in the garden and I could hear you talking. Alison told me you'd be back for the whole summer. Is that true?'

Leila said, 'As far as we can tell. For now.'

'That's great.' Rosie smiled and enthused, charming and insincere. 'I've just moved back from London. Couldn't afford to live there anymore. Owed thousands on plastic.' She glanced back towards her house, 'Actually, Alison thinks it was just hundreds, so keep that to yourselves.' She turned to me then, and said, 'I'm sorry. I can't remember your name.'

'Olivia.'

She smiled at me. 'That's right,' she said, 'I think we've met before.'

I looked away.

Over on the terrace, in the shade of the gazebo, Grace was colouring in pictures with her usual artistic abandon, and Katherine flicked through magazines full of play houses and trampolines for the garden. Lily was asleep indoors, and a baby monitor stood on the table beside her. I'd noticed her watching Rosie as she approached us.

Grace jumped down from her seat and ran over to us, then sat on the edge of Leila's sunbed and handed her a picture. 'Look. I made you this.'

Leila took it and smiled. 'Thank you.'

'It's a bus,' Grace added, helpfully.

Rosie said, 'Is that your sister?'

'Half-sister.'

Grace looked up at Rosie curiously. Rosie ignored her. She fumbled in her bag and brought out a packet of cigarettes. She put one between her lips and was about to light it, when Leila said, 'We can't smoke here. Sorry. Not around the kids.'

'Crap.' Rosie dropped her cigarette on the ground, then said, 'And I suppose we're not supposed to swear, either.'

Leila shook her head.

For a while there was silence. Katherine stood up from her seat beneath the gazebo and called out to Grace to come inside.

Grace didn't move or answer her. She leant forwards and said to Leila,

'I think I'll just stay here.'

Katherine's voice grew louder. 'Grace!'

Rosie watched, and looked amused.

Frowning, Katherine strode over to us. She grabbed Grace by the hand and pulled her up. Grace snivelled. 'I want to stay here.'

Leila said, 'It's all right. She can stay with us if she wants to.'

Katherine pursed her lips. 'I don't think so, Leila. Thank you.'

Rosie stood up. She moved forwards towards Katherine. 'I'm sorry. I've been rude. How are you?'

'I'm well, thank you, Rosie.'

Rosie smiled. She reached out and laid a hand over Katherine's bare stomach. 'Alison tells me you're expecting another boy.'

Katherine stepped backwards. Rosie's hand fell.

Rosie continued. 'That's wonderful news, isn't it? After Alfie. And after having two girls. You must be very happy.'

'Yes.'

'And now, finally, someone can fill Alfie's place.'

Katherine turned around. She took Grace's hand again and walked her back to the house. I looked at Rosie as she sat back down. Beneath the hair that had fallen over her face, she was still smiling.

•

In the middle of the night, once everyone else was asleep, Leila came into my room. She switched on the lamp beside the bed and crawled in next to me, curling her body around mine. We'd hardly slept together since we arrived here. I wasn't sure whether she was conscious of her father in the room next to mine, or if it might have been more than that. Being here was hard for her. Seeing Katherine and her belly full of baby, and the family that had gone on and on without her all these years was like living through the past again, but worse now, because the hope had gone. They sent her away when she was nine and grieving, and there was nothing anyone could do anymore with those years. They were just going to drift around her history, surfacing now and then, unexpectedly, full of new ways to hurt her.

I felt her breath on my neck as she whispered, 'Are you asleep?'

I rolled over and faced her. 'No.'

She pressed her lips against mine. I reached for her and responded. My hands held her, moving over her flesh, warm and familiar. I longed for her. I laid my hands against the bare skin of her thighs, and then moved to kiss her between them. She pulled away.

For a while, we were silent. I felt the stinging threat of tears, and closed my eyes to stop them falling.

She said, 'Sorry.'

I said, 'What's wrong?'

'Nothing.' Then, after a moment, she said, 'I hate it here.'

Her voice in the dark was hollow and lonely.

I asked, 'Is it because of Katherine?'

'You like her.' I caught the reproach in her voice.

'She's not as bad as I thought she was going to be.' Then I asked, 'Why do you hate her so much?'

'You know this story.'

I thought, *No I don't. I hardly know anything. You shut me out and refuse to speak. All I know is that a baby died and you were sent to school afterwards because Katherine didn't want to look after a child that wasn't hers.*

I said, 'I wonder whether she did it all deliberately. Perhaps she just went mad for a while.'

Leila spoke slowly. I wished I could see her face. 'No,' she said. 'She wasn't mad. And I don't hate her. But there are too many memories here for me. Just here in this room, there are so many things I want to forget.'

I thought, *That's your problem. You work to forget everything. You want to blot out half your life. Just remember it, and move on.*

I said, 'We can leave, if it's making you unhappy.'

'No.'

She took my hand then, and held it against her cheek. But that was all.

•

The baby was born at home two days later. We went away that night. The next day, when we came back, the village was deserted. Everyone was worn out with the summer's relentless heat. They stayed inside and shut their curtains against the sun. The news was warning of worse to come.

The only person who seemed to be outside was Grace. She was in the front garden when we arrived, sitting on the edge of her paddling pool. Four or five Barbie dolls floated face down in the water. She looked up as we walked along the path from the gate. She smelled sweetly of suncream. Leila stooped and said hello.

'The baby's been born,' Grace announced.

Leila smiled. 'That's why we came back. We wanted to see him.'

'You'll have to ask dad. Mum won't let you. She told him.'

Her five-year-old boldness astounded me.

Leila kept her tone casual. 'Really? Why's that?'

Grace shrugged. 'I don't know. She just doesn't like you.' She paused for a moment while she fished a naked, drowned-looking Barbie out of the paddling pool. 'But I do, so you can have this doll if you want. But not to keep. Just to borrow.'

Leila took it and smiled. 'Thanks.'

We went inside. Grace called after us, 'He's got a very pointy head and he's not very handsome.'

Gus and Katherine were together in the front room. As soon as we walked in, Gus stood up and carried the baby to Leila and put him in her arms. She sat down in an armchair and traced one finger over his cheek. He moved his face towards her. She laughed. 'He likes me.'

'Reflexes,' Katherine corrected, tersely.

Brightly, I asked, 'What's his name?'

Katherine smiled at me. 'Isaac.'

I looked at Leila from the corner of my eye. She was staring down at the baby, lying asleep in her arms. I couldn't read her expression, but I knew I could see no joy there.

V

Leila

It stayed light outside for longer by now. In the field opposite our house were four newborn lambs. The farmer had told me he expected hundreds, but these were the earliest. I liked watching them from my window, stretched out on the grass with their curly white fleeces drying off in the sun.

Rosie and I spent all our time together. Years later, Olivia asked me why I'd done it – stayed friends with her despite her cruelty. I had no answer, other than that I was locked into it. She might have been cruel, but she was also my only friend, and I depended on her. She came with all the appeal of the exotic.

At school, now I longer saw the woman with all her broken dolls, I did extra reading with a new woman who came in on Thursdays. The books were usually classics. I entered a dream world full of balls and steam trains and girls who did school work on slates. Perhaps the staff thought this would help me. Perhaps not. It helped me later on, though, once I was away at school, in the days before Olivia.

Katherine still spent most of her time at home. She'd relaxed into motherhood. She didn't cry anymore. In fact, for that short time, she and my father were genuinely, tangibly happy. Joy hung off them like a disease I was expected to catch.

It was March. The clocks were going forwards, and it would soon be summer again. Rosie and I were going for a picnic in the woods. My father trusted Rosie.

She was eleven now, and I was nine. Responsible.

My father was making us sandwiches. Rosie asked, 'Can we take Alfie with us on our picnic?'

He laughed, 'No. Absolutely not. Sorry, Rosie.'

I took my bag down from where it hung on the kitchen door. My father handed me a plastic box full of sandwiches and crisps and cheese, and an old rug that I'd found in the airing cupboard. There was also an apple, cut in two, already turning slowly brown. We were meant to share it. They battled to make me eat fruit.

I said goodbye to my father. He kissed me and told me to be careful, and to make sure I was back by two. I looked at my watch. It was half past twelve. The watch was a present from my father, the day before Alfie came home, when we'd gone shopping to buy everything for his nursery. (Katherine wouldn't buy anything before he was born. Superstition.) It was silver, and when I went outside and the sun shone on it, the light bounced off the face and created a white star in the air. It didn't just tell you the time. It told you the date as well.

Rosie followed me out through the front door. At the end of the garden path, we had to cross the lane and climb over the fence to the orchard, next to the field where all the lambs were. The ewes stared at us as we trudged over the grass and the mud. One stamped her black feet, and strange warning noises came from her throat.

Rosie said, 'Why wouldn't your dad let us bring the baby?'

'I don't know. He has to stay at home so Katherine can feed him. And we might drop him, or lose him.'

'That'd be funny.'

She linked her arm through mine and we walked on. At the furthest end of the orchard, a path led down to the woods. Nettles and bramble bushes grew at the side.

I pricked my finger as I tried to untangle the branches that overhung the pathway. A tiny dot of blood appeared. I sucked it away. It tasted of dirty silver.

Inside the wood it was dark. The trees shut out the sun. The ground under our feet was brown and littered with fallen twigs and hazel catkins. Before, when I'd come here with my father, the air had been soaked with the smell of wild garlic. It had been summer then, and the leaves were full and green. Now everything just smelled wet and fresh, and the trees and plants were bare.

The branches creaked. We could hear falling twigs and leaves all around us. They made their own private storm we couldn't see. There were animals scratching their way through the bracken and sometimes I caught sight of a grey squirrel or a rabbit hurrying through the undergrowth. Rosie took my hand, and we walked further on through the trees towards a clearing. I'd been there before with my father. Possibly also my mother. It carried the ring of the deeply familiar.

It was grassy in the clearing, and full of white and yellow daffodils and holes the rabbits had made. At the edge ran a stream. Rosie stood still and looked around and said, 'Let's eat our lunch here.'

We sat in the shadow of a willow tree, growing on the bank of the stream. I untied the string on my bag and took out the box with our food in it, then spread the rug over the ground beside us. Some rooks started calling in the trees overhead.

Then, on the other side of the stream among the bushes, I saw a deer, standing among the bracken with its fawn.

I nudged Rosie and whispered, 'Look,' but before Rosie turned around, the deer and its baby had fled, darting silently into the undergrowth.

We began to eat. The sun now was warm and strong. Rosie took her jumper off. Beneath it she wore just a t-shirt, and under that I could see the white strap of a bra. I wondered when she'd started wearing it.

Rosie said, 'You're looking at my tits.'

I blushed. 'No, I'm not.'

'It doesn't matter.'

She leant back on her arms so her chest stuck out further. I carried on eating. I liked the noise the stream made as it flowed over the rocks. I said, 'Shall we go in the stream?'

'OK.'

We abandoned our lunch things on the rug and walked down the bank to the edge. The water in the stream ran clear, moving rapidly over brown and orange stones. I knelt down and skimmed the surface with my hand. I saw a tiny grey fish, whirling away in the current.

We kicked our shoes and socks off. Rosie was the first to go in. She laughed. 'It's really cold.' The water swirled around the bottom of her jeans.

I turned up my trousers before wading in. I sunk my hand under the water and held it there, to see if I could feel it turning cold when it chilled the blood in my wrist, where the veins lay closest to the surface of my skin. I'd learned about it last week, when we were studying science.

Suddenly, Rosie cupped her hands and started splashing the water into my face. It was so cold it made me gasp. I turned my head away. 'Stop it!' I yelled, although I laughed, too.

Rosie tossed her hair. 'You're such a baby. Don't be afraid of a little bit of water. Look.' And she lay down on her front in the stream.

I stood on the rocks and stared at her. I could see her starting to shiver.

She kicked her legs and laughed. 'Come on. Lie down.'

So I did. I lowered myself in slowly at first, crawling down on all fours and kneeling on the stones at the bottom. Then, gradually, I hovered my stomach over the water and stretched out until I was lying flat like Rosie.

I grinned, and shivered.

Rosie said, 'Don't worry. It gets warmer after a while.'

I moved around from side to side to warm up. Among the ripples I made, I noticed the branch of a silver birch tree reflected in the water. I stopped moving, and traced my fingers through it. The year before, when I'd been on holiday to Cornwall with my father, we'd stayed in a cottage near the beach, and at night I could look out of the window and see the image of the moon shining on the sea, like a path leading all the way to the horizon. I used to wonder what would happen if I sneaked outside and swam out over it, and what I might find if I ever reached the end of the moon's path. My father said it would only lead to more darkness, because in winter, no matter where I was, I'd only ever be following the night.

I looked down at my watch. The second hand had stopped. I shook my wrist and held it to my ear to listen for the sounds of clockwork inside. There was nothing. When I looked at the face again, I could see tiny bubbles of water underneath the glass. I stood up. My clothes were soaking wet. They stuck to my body and made me shiver. 'My watch has broken,' I said, and I heard the quiver in my voice.

'I need to get out and mend it.'

Rosie came with me out of the water. Under her t-shirt, her bra had gone see-through and I could see the small round swelling of her breasts. We picked up our shoes and socks from the water's edge, then Rosie took my hand and we climbed back up the bank to the willow tree. My clothes grew even colder as the air hit them, and when we sat down on the grass my teeth chattered and my body shook from the cold.

I took my watch off and laid it on the ground, in a patch where the sun was shining. 'It needs to dry before we go home,' I said. 'Does yours still work?'

Rosie looked at her watch. 'Yes. It's fine. Mine's waterproof.' She showed it to me. One-fifteen. Then she reached for the blanket we'd left on the grass. 'I'm freezing.'

'So am I.'

'If we take our clothes off, we can wrap this around us and we'll get much warmer.'

I hesitated. I looked around, to see if anyone was coming, then I said, 'OK,' and took off my jumper and trousers. I wrapped the rug around my shoulders and curled my knees up to my chest.

'That's not fair. I need some.'

Rosie took off her jeans and t-shirt, and I held out the rug so she could sit under it with me. We sat like that for a few minutes, then Rosie said, 'Let's play a game.'

'OK.'

'Let's pretend Alfie is our baby and we've left him at home with a babysitter.'

'That's boring.'

'No, it's not. We're eighteen. We never wanted a child, so we've gone off and left him, so we can have sex for the day.'

She lay down on the ground and covered herself with the rug. She reached up and put her hand on my bare back, and ran it up and down my spine.

'Come on. Lay down beside me.'

I giggled, and stayed sitting up. Rosie carried on running her fingers all over my back.

'Lay down,' she said again, but this time her voice was a whisper.

I curled up on the ground at her side. We stayed like that for a while, until Rosie's eyes closed and she moved her face closer to mine, and began to kiss my lips, the way I'd seen my father do with Katherine.

I stayed still. Rosie still spoke in her low voice and said, 'Open your mouth and kiss me back.'

So I did, and Rosie's tongue on mine felt warm and soft.

•

She stayed over that night. My father took the mattress off one of the spare beds and carried it into the attic over his shoulder. It was an old mattress, with a rusty-coloured stain in the middle that looked like spilt tea, and springs inside that creaked when you laid down. We covered it with a white sheet from the airing cupboard and Rosie went home and came back with her sleeping bag. It was dark blue and covered with yellow stars and moons, like a night sky.

My watch still wasn't working. I'd hidden it in my secret chest, so my father wouldn't find out. I had to look at the alarm clock beside my bed now instead, and work out which buttons to press when I needed to wind the time forwards in the middle of the night. My father told me the clocks would be changing at two in the morning, and I wanted to stay up and see if the night became darker as the world skipped an hour.

Rosie lay on the mattress on my floor. I didn't have a television in my room like she did, so we read our books instead, and talked while we waited for the night to fall, so my father would bring up our midnight feast. After tonight, it wouldn't be getting dark until later in the evenings, and then the months would wear on and it would be the summer solstice, when it hardly grew dark at all. That was the day I would be turning nine-and-a-half.

I looked up from my book and smiled at Rosie. Downstairs, Alfie was crying.

Rosie was reading a magazine which she threw on the floor. 'That baby's crying again.'

'I know.'

'Shall we go and see him?'

'If you like.'

We went downstairs in our pyjamas. I poked my head around my father's bedroom door. He was sitting on the edge of the bed, trying to soothe the baby and get him to sleep.

Rosie walked over to him. She put her adult voice on. 'Do you think it would be OK if I held the baby?'

'Sure. Just one moment.'

She sat down on the floor and he handed Alfie to her. She held him in her lap and looked down at him. After a while, he stopped crying and he stared at her. She looked up at me and smiled.

•

Afterwards, my father laid the baby in his basket and wound up the mobile that played lullaby music. He shut the curtains to keep out the light, then we left the room and he went downstairs to sit with Katherine and watch television and drink wine.

The music drifted out from the bedroom, and Rosie wandered off the landing and into the nursery. I followed her. The window had been left slightly open, even though it wasn't cold. The Peter Rabbit curtains blew in the wind, although the room wasn't cold. Alfie's cot stood in the corner. He didn't sleep in it yet because he was too young. It was the cot that used to be mine. My father had taken it from the cellar and washed it and put it back together one day. I tried sometimes to imagine myself sleeping in there as a baby, and my mother caring for me the way Katherine cared for Alfie. I wondered whether her fingerprints might still be on the wood, or if my father would have washed them all away.

Rosie tiptoed over the floorboards and opened one of the drawers in the chest.

She sounded disappointed. 'Why are they all empty?'

'Some aren't.' I opened the top two drawers. They were full of babygros and tops and trousers. 'They mostly keep everything in their room.'

'Will he sleep in here tonight?'

'I don't know. Sometimes they put him in here when they go to bed and sometimes they leave him with them. It all depends.'

'On what?'

'I'm not all that sure.'

'It's because they do it at night and they don't want him to watch.'

'It is not.'

'I bet you it is. If you come down one night when he's sleeping in here, you'll be able to hear the noises they make when they're doing it.' She paused for a moment then said, 'I bet Katherine really hams it up.'

I picked up a toy elephant from on top of the drawers. I knew the noises Rosie was talking about. She meant murmurs and sighs, like the ones she'd been making that afternoon when we were in the wood. I'd never done that before, and I knew it was a secret, to be kept from my father and all the children at my school.

Rosie walked over to the cot. There were no blankets inside it, just a plastic mattress covered with a soft white sheet that felt like fleece when you touched it. She said, 'What time does your dad go to bed?'

'I don't know. But they don't stay up really late, because of the baby.'

'If they put him in here, we can come down in the night and take him.'

I shook my head. 'No, we can't. They've got a baby monitor, and if my dad heard us, he'd go mad.'

'We'll be careful. He won't cry. We'll take him up to your room.'

I put the toy elephant back on the chest of drawers. 'I suppose we could, if they bring him in here to sleep, but we'll have to bring him back down. We can't keep him all night.'

Rosie put her arm around my shoulders. 'We can do whatever we like,' she said. 'He's ours.'

•

At midnight, the church bells chimed twelve. It was easier to hear them at night, because everything was so silent. I imagined my mother's grave, lying in the garden in the shadow of the church. I knew her body would have rotted away by now, her bones just dust in the earth. But her soul was somewhere else. No one could see her, but she was always there, looking at what was happening in the family she'd left behind.

When the church bells stopped, Rosie said, 'Let's go and see if the baby's in the nursery.'

Everything below us was silent. Katherine and my father had gone to bed two hours ago.

I said, 'He might not be there. He might be in their room.'

'Let's go and see, anyway.'

I looked around the room. 'What will we do when we've got him?'

She raised her head and looked at me squarely. She said, 'We'll send him up to your mother.'

'How?'

'I'm not sure yet. But we will. You know she wants him.'

'OK.'

'And then Katherine will stop being so cruel, and stop trying to get rid of you by giving your dad new babies.'

We tiptoed downstairs as quietly as we could. I was shaking. If we carried it out, our plan would involve killing the baby. I understood that much. From then on, Rosie only called him *The fucking baby*. That was what she'd called him during the game we'd played earlier, when we talked about him in the woods. She never used his name again. I felt heady and excited and sick.

The door to the nursery was half open and a dim yellow light fell over the floorboards, cast by the lamp on the chest of drawers. I bent my head around the door and looked in. The cot was empty.

I turned round and whispered, 'He's not here.'

'He must be,' Rosie said, and there was desperation in her voice. She pushed me into the room.

Once inside, I saw the moses basket by the window. They hadn't put him in the cot. They'd just brought his bed in here.

Rosie crept towards him. She took long strides across the floor instead of tiptoeing normally. It took less time, and made less noise. I stood by the baby monitor on the windowsill. As long as we were quiet, I knew my father wouldn't hear us. Alfie had a white noise machine, which made the sounds of the sea and sent the noise back through the monitor to my father's room. It was only when Alfie cried that you could hear him.

Rosie said, 'Now let's take him upstairs.'

And she lowered her hands into the basket and picked him up.

He didn't wake up, although sometimes it looked as though he were about to. I was afraid that my father or Katherine would come in and find us. I said, 'Let's put him back. Let's put him back before he cries.'

'He won't cry.'

'He might.'

We kept him upstairs with us until the church bells chimed again and the numbers on the clock said 12.15. Rosie yawned and said, 'You put him back. I'm too tired to go downstairs.'

I looked at him lying in my arms and asked, 'Is he OK?'

'Of course he is. He's fine. Don't worry. It was only a game. We haven't done anything.'

I took him back down to the nursery and laid him down in his basket.

•

When I went back upstairs, Rosie looked as though she were asleep, although I suspected she might be pretending. I said, 'Are you awake?' She stayed silent.

It was late now and I was tired, but I still wanted to stay awake and see what would happen at two o'clock, when the time went forwards. Before I got back into bed, I opened the secret chest and took out my broken watch. It still said five to one, and the date was stuck at the 23rd of March. I shook it again to see if the hands would start moving, but they didn't, so I put it back down on top of the envelope with Alfie's hair in it. Beneath the envelope still lay the photographs of my mother and Alfie, clipped together. I took them out, and decided to sleep with them under my pillow.

I climbed back into bed. On the floor beside me, Rosie slept. I looked at the photo of my mother, then tucked it under the pillow and turned out the light. The room didn't go completely dark because of the full moon shining above the skylight.

I closed my eyes, but I could still see my mother's face among the black, as though a strange, shadowy portrait of her had been left on the inside of my eyelids.

When I opened my eyes again, the clock beside the bed said 1.54. I sat up and watched as the minutes passed and the numbers changed, until finally it was 1.59.

Then I decided to count, and as I grew closer to sixty, I raised my head and looked up out of the skylight.

Nothing happened. There was only the faint sound of the trees shifting in the breeze. I changed the time on my clock to 3.00, but the church bells only chimed two.

I laid back down again and wondered what would happen now to the hour that had been lost. Perhaps the rustling of the trees had been the noise the hour made as it rushed into the night and away off the face of the earth. Yesterday, my father had said the hour wouldn't really be lost. The clocks would change again in winter, and this time they would go backwards and the hour would come back to us. I wasn't sure. I wondered whether all the lost hours since the world began were being stored somewhere, and you'd find them again when you went to heaven. That was why people could go on living after they'd died – because of all the hours that had been saved up for them.

I went to sleep with that thought lodged quite comfortably in my mind.

•

In the morning, Alfie was dead. Rosie and I were in the kitchen. We heard Katherine scream, and then she called my father, again and again and again.

I looked at him, and saw all the colour drain from his face until even his lips were grey. It made me feel sick. He threw his mug on the worktop and ran away upstairs. The grandfather clock chimed seven. They'd been pleased he'd slept so long.

Rosie pushed her chair away from the table. 'I have to go home.'

We could hear them in the nursery. I clasped my hands together and felt my eyes fill with tears. 'I think something's wrong with the baby.'

'I know.'

'Don't go yet. Stay here until he's better.'

Rosie shook her head. She was still wearing her pyjamas, and didn't have any shoes. 'I have to go home,' she said again. Without turning to look at me, she walked out through the back door and away down the path.

I sat still. I was too afraid to go upstairs. Someone up there was crying. It wasn't like ordinary crying. It was fierce and bleak, and it seemed to be going on and on and on.

•

The kettle that my father had left on the stove boiled and whistled. I took it off the heat and stood it on the cooling pad beside it. Alfie was dead. I knew, even though no one had told me. I knew from the way Katherine screamed. And now I didn't really know what to do, so I decided to sit back down at the table and finish my Coco Pops.

I chewed each mouthful for a long time. Every time I swallowed it sent a shudder through my body. I looked out of the window. Everything was normal.

My father came back into the kitchen. He was sombre-faced and shaking. He stood in front of me and said they needed to take the baby to hospital, and that I was to take myself round to Rosie's until he came to pick me up. Then he ran out into the hall where Katherine was waiting for him, and together they ran out to the car with Alfie in Katherine's arms, wrapped up in a blanket, silent and rigid as china.

I went upstairs. The nursery door had been left open, but I didn't go inside. I carried on up to my bedroom and dressed in my jeans and a blue jumper. I took the photos of my mother and Alfie out from under my pillow and locked them back in the secret chest. Rosie's clothes and sleeping bag were still lying on the floor by the mattress she'd slept on. I gathered them in my arms and carried them downstairs.

I walked out of the kitchen and onto the garden path, then over the gravel to Rosie's house. She opened the door. She took her things out of my arms and said,

'Where's your dad?'

'He took Alfie to hospital. He wants me to come here until they get home.'

Rosie shook her head. 'You can't. No one's in. I'm going out in a minute.'

'But he…'

'You can't come in. You'll have to go home and wait for them there. Sorry.'

And she stepped back inside and closed the door.

I turned around and walked back over the gravel to my house. My chest felt hard and heavy. I wished it were a school day, or yesterday, or any day but this one. At the bottom of the garden path I stopped walking. The house in front of me looked cold and frightening. It was too big to go back to alone. I went through the gate and into the front garden. The day wasn't cold, so I pulled back the branches of the fir trees and stepped inside the hollow. Then I laid down on the ground by my doll's grave, to wait there until my father came home.

VI

Olivia

Finally, rain shattered the heat. For over half an hour it fell, heavy and abundant. It felt luxurious. The trees and the garden stopped dying of thirst.

Outside, the day was dark. I sat upstairs in my room while the rain hammered the windowpanes. Leila was out with Gus. Last week, he'd bought her a car and was teaching her to drive. She said she was finding it hard, though whether she meant the driving or the hours spent in a confined space with her father was unclear.

We only had a month left here. Another month in limbo. That was the trouble with this summer. Neither of us was anywhere solid. We were just floating through time on our way somewhere else. Rotherfield Hall was over, but nothing else had begun, and the past and the future were becoming distant, far-off places I couldn't imagine being in, though there were times recently when I'd been longing for the past. I'd been longing for its return as though it were an absent lover. In many ways, it was. It had disappeared, and taken her with it.

I didn't know what was wrong with her, but I put it all down to Ash Farm.

She'd taken one of the photos of Alfie from the mantelpiece in my room. I didn't know why, or what she'd done with it. She hardly came in here anymore. Often these days, I found myself looking at her and wondering what was happening in her head. I thought I'd like to read her mind, but even if I could get inside it, I knew I'd find nothing as simple as a narrative. I'd find a web, still being spun, and I'd become trapped in it like a fly, just as everyone else here had been. There was no way out of your own story. You stayed in it, floundering, holding out for a decent end.

I stood and looked at the photo of her as a child, holding Alfie in her arms the day before he died. She was smiling. It was hard to imagine that a few hours later, her life was to be overwhelmed, and altered forever.

'Olivia.'

I turned round, surprised, expecting to see Katherine. Rosie stood in the doorway. She wore a red dress and red shoes. She smiled, and came in. 'Katherine said you were up here.' She sat down on the bed, hooked one leg over the other, and looked at me for a moment, then she said, 'How are you finding it?'

'What?'

She gestured extravagantly, taking in the room and everything beyond it. 'This,' she said. 'Being here.'

'Fine.'

'Leila seems very happy to be back.'

I thought, *How do you know? You hardly know her anymore. You've barely seen her in the last eight years.* But I stopped myself, because she did know. She knew the child in the photograph. She was right there with her on the night the baby died. The thought made me feel powerless, and excluded. If nothing else, the shared experience of a dead baby would be a bond between two people – one that I could never compete with.

She picked up the photo of Leila and me beside the bed. 'This is nice,' she said.

I smiled thinly.

She went on. 'You two are very close.'

'We're good friends.'

'Are you gay?'

'Sorry?'

'You and Leila. Are you gay?'

'No.'

'Liar. It's all right. I won't tell anyone.'

I shrugged. 'Whatever.'

'So you are, then?'

'I really don't see why this is any of your business.'

She leaned back on the bed. Her dress had risen to her thighs. Her tone when she spoke again was final. 'So you are.'

I looked away from her, picked some books up off the floor and filed them away on the shelf. The rest of the room was immaculate. I had nothing to do but listen to Rosie.

She said, 'What do you think of Katherine?'

'Actually, I think she's very nice.'

'Leila hates her.'

I hesitated. 'I'm not sure about that. I think things have been difficult for them. For all of them.'

'You're very diplomatic. I think you must have an opinion. Do you know what happened?'

I shrugged. 'Yes.'

'Who do you believe?'

'What do you mean?'

'Whose side are you on?' she asked simply. 'Leila's or Katherine's?'

I said nothing.

She shrugged. 'Suit yourself. But you know, Leila hasn't been home for years. Alison, my mother, thinks things are going to become very strained, particularly now the baby's here. You might start wishing you'd never come.'

'I doubt that.'

'Has Leila ever told you what happened that night when Alfie died?'

'She doesn't like talking about it.'

She stood up and came close to me. I stepped back.

She lowered her voice sympathetically. 'You're very loyal, Olivia. You don't want to believe anything bad about your friend.'

I continued to say nothing, but her words rocked me.

She rested her hand lightly on my arm. 'You're a lovely girl. That's obvious,' she said. 'But look after yourself here. My mother calls this house a nest of vipers, and she's right. Gus and Katherine are miserable, and you might think you know Leila…'

'I really don't need to listen to this.'

'OK. If that's what you think. I'm just warning you.' Her tone became low and intimate. 'I'm only next door if you ever want to get away.' And she leaned forwards and kissed me lightly on the mouth.

•

After she'd gone, I went downstairs and joined Katherine. She was sitting in the rocking chair in the kitchen, breastfeeding Isaac while Lily painted indeterminate pictures at the table.

She smiled at me as I went in. 'Hi, Liv. Are you bored?'

I sat down beside Lily and absent-mindedly picked up a brush and dipped it in red paint. 'No,' I said. I looked at the brush in my hand, 'I felt like painting.'

She laughed. 'What did Rosie want?'

'God knows.'

'You don't like her much.'

'I think she's the most revolting person I've ever met. And that's quite hard, considering some of the girls who went to our school.' At Rotherfield, tongue-sharpening had been an art, or at the very least, a survival skill. It became a weapon most girls carried with them into adulthood, hidden discreetly behind glossy lips, white teeth and the tenderest of smiles. I wondered about Katherine as she sat opposite me, her baby draining her breast. The epitome of selfless maternal devotion, who had sent Leila away for a crime she'd never committed.

She said, 'You're probably right about that. She's always been unpleasant. Even as a child she was fairly obnoxious, but you could make allowances for it then. A sad past can excuse a lot, up to a certain age.'

I wondered whether she was aware of any irony as she spoke. She obviously thought people should stop making allowances once a child had passed nine.

I said, 'Leila told me she was quite cruel.'

'I'm sure she was. But Leila herself…' She thought better of it then, and stopped.

The back door opened, and Leila and Gus came in. Katherine focussed her attention on the baby, unlatching him from her breast and sitting him on her lap to wind him. His head lolled into his chest.

Leila addressed her father. 'Can I hold him?'

Gus said, 'Of course.'

Katherine said, 'No.'

He rolled his eyes heavenward. 'For God's sake.'

From her place in the rocking chair, Katherine glared at him. He ignored her. Leila looked from one to the other. She said, 'I'm not here to hurt anyone.'

They all carried on in silence, ignoring the words that had finally been spoken, still hanging like balloons in the air.

VII

Leila

Behind the clouds, the sun was slipping further away. It left only a few streaks behind it, which purpled the sky above the fir trees. The day was ending, and still no one came home.

I stood up from the ground by the doll's grave and rubbed my eyes. I wondered whether I'd been asleep. My hair was full of pine needles, and my clothes were dirty. Perhaps my father had already been back and hadn't seen me, hidden by myself in the hollow.

I pulled back the branches and stepped out into the garden. The evening was growing cold, and I shivered.

All the windows of the house were dark. I knew it must still be empty. I walked up to the kitchen window overlooking the front garden and peered inside. Everything was just as they'd left it this morning. The table was set for breakfast, and the metal handle of my spoon still poked over the edge of my bowl. One of Alfie's bibs and a blanket were lying on the worktop by the coffee machine, waiting for him to come downstairs.

I turned away and unlatched the gate that took me round the edge of the house, through the side door and inside. It was darker than it had been out in the garden.

The house felt empty. As I stood by myself in the kitchen, it felt to me as though hundreds of years had passed since anyone lived there, and I'd just stumbled in and found it, dusty and dirty, and full of secrets.

I tiptoed over to the worktop. Katherine's mug of tea stood there, half-drunk. I stuck the tip of my finger in it. It was cold and milky. Beside it, the coffee machine was still switched on, with the lamp lit to say it was ready. My father's cup stood on the steel tray underneath. I pressed the button at the front. The machine droned and gurgled, and a long trickle of dark-smelling coffee fell down into the mug. I pressed it again and it stopped. I took the mug away and covered it with a teacloth, to keep it warm until he came home.

I looked down at Alfie's bib and his blanket. The bib was white, and had a picture of a bear on the front. The blanket was folded into a square. Katherine had only just washed it, and she'd taken it out of the airing cupboard this morning, ready to wrap around him when she brought him downstairs and fed him.

I picked up the bib and the blanket and held them both against my cheek. Then I took them away to my room.

•

It was Katherine who came home first. I was back down in the kitchen by then, rocking in the rocking chair. She came in through the side door, looking pale and ill.

She sat down on a chair at the end of the table. Her eyes were big and dark. She smiled faintly, but when she spoke her voice was hoarse. 'We thought you were at Rosie's. Your dad's gone to pick you up.'

I looked at the floor. 'No one was in.'

Katherine nodded.

I said, 'Where's Alfie?'

There was silence for a while, then she knelt on the floor in front of me and took my hands, and spoke again in her hoarse whisper. 'Alfie's dead, Leila,' she said.

•

My father came home. His eyes were pink and his face stained. I stood up and took the mug of coffee from underneath the teacloth. It was still warm, so I passed it to him. 'I made you this.'

He smiled. 'Thank you.'

It amazed me that they could smile and yet feel so sad.

Everyone was quiet again. Katherine's gaze darted around the room. 'Where's his blanket?'

My father sighed. 'I don't know.'

Katherine slumped into a chair by the window. Her voice was no longer hoarse, but it sounded strange and far away. 'I gave the other ones to the nurses. I can't bear the idea of him getting cold in the night, shut in that room all by himself.' She lifted her head then, and stared at my father. 'I don't know how we can do this. I don't know how we can get through the next forty or fifty years without ever seeing him again.'

My father said nothing. He just shook his head. I wondered why no one was crying.

•

Later, a policeman dressed in jeans and driving an unmarked car came to inspect the nursery. My father and Katherine were downstairs in the living room, barely speaking. The house was bleak. I was afraid of every room. My attic was too far away, but downstairs felt desolate. I dangled about the landing instead, near the policeman searching the nursery. For a while, I stood in the doorway. He smiled at me as he picked up the baby monitor and wrote what he saw in his notebook. He had a brown leather bag with him, and he took the sheets and a soft toy out of the basket, wrapped them up in plastic and put them inside it.

I wanted to ask what he was doing. I felt sick. Images from the night before infested my head. I worked to push them away.

•

I had the week off school and my father stayed home from work. Katherine spent most of her time in bed with the curtains shut and the door closed. No one went into the nursery. No one went in there for years.

There had to be a post-mortem. Once that was over, there could be a funeral. Alfie would lie in a white coffin lined with lace. They offered me the choice. I could go, or stay at home. I could stay at home with Rosie.

For days and weeks, I was simply aware of stillness and disbelief. And fear. The enormity of his death hovered in the air all around us, but there was no way to make it penetrate. There never was. Years later, Katherine was still looking for him.

In the earliest days, Rosie's mother was their main support. She carried round boxes full of food that she'd made, so no one would need to worry about cooking. She helped with the funeral arrangements when my father and Katherine were too dazed to do it themselves. And she took me off their hands for days on end.

Rosie hardly spoke to me, or looked at me. Once, when I said to her, 'Are you OK?' she said, 'I can't believe he died.'

I sat on her living room floor and traced the pattern in the carpet with my fingertip. 'Some babies die for no reason. That's what my dad said.'

'They do not. No one dies for no reason. They have to be ill first. Something must have happened to him.'

I looked at her and said, 'A doctor's going to have a look, to try and work it out.'

I wanted to hear panic in her voice. She said, 'A look at the baby?'

'Yes.'

'Will they cut him open, and see his heart and his brain?'

I shrugged. I didn't know. 'I don't think so. That'd be disgusting.'

'It doesn't mean they wouldn't do it.' She paused. 'Will they definitely find out how he died?'

'Yes.'

Rosie turned away from me. 'Well, you'd better start worrying, then,' she said.

'Why?'

'Because we both know what happened, Leila. Don't pretend. He died because you killed him.'

•

After the post-mortem, I went home. Katherine was in bed again. My father showed me a gift the hospital had given them. It was a piece of clay with two baby footprints pressed into it. At the top, someone had carved the year, and underneath the footprints in neat curly letters it said Alfred Hartley, with the date that he'd been born and the date that he'd died.

My father sat beside me. He said, 'The funeral will be soon. But the doctors couldn't work out why Alfie died, so we need to have an inquest.'

I nodded. I had no idea what an inquest was, but it sounded grave, and I was afraid. I said, 'Why couldn't they work it out?'

My father hesitated for a moment, as if weighing up whether it was right to tell me. Then he said, 'They think he suffocated in his sleep, and they need to find out what made him suffocate.'

'Did someone kill him?'

'No. Of course not. No one killed him. That's why we need to have an inquest.'

•

A policeman came round and attacked me with questions.

- Did you see Alfie the night before he died?

- Did he usually sleep with toys in his bed?'

- Do either of your parents smoke?'

- Do you like your step-mother?'

- Do you think your step-mother was happy when she'd had the baby?'

- Really?'

- Have you ever seen her cry?'

- What about after the baby was born?'

- Really? Could you tell me a little more about that?'

- Do you think she lost her temper when the baby cried like that?'

- And how was she in the days afterwards?

- Thank you for talking to us, Leila.

He gave me a bar of chocolate from his bag.

•

The inquest opened after a week and was adjourned. The police still came round. They still asked questions. I understood, though no one told me, that Katherine was suspected of killing him.

The atmosphere in the house was dark and thick. Katherine wept. I'd never seen anyone so upset, or angry. A journalist from the local paper came round. She swore at him. Later, she howled. She was raw, made up of nothing but grief.

I spent most of my time in my room. When they had the energy, my father and Katherine were furious with me because the police had spoken to Rosie, and our stories didn't match. She hadn't lied like I had. She'd told them about taking him out of his bed in the middle of the night. She'd told them we had him upstairs in the attic, and that was the last time she'd seen him.

The night before the funeral, Katherine came up to my room. She asked me questions about what we'd done with the baby. She said, 'Did you hurt him, Leila?'

I said, 'No.'

She said, 'Did you put the soft toy in his bed when you took him downstairs?'

I said, 'Yes.'

She looked away from me and took deep breaths. I could see her shoulders hunched over and shaking and thought she must be crying. She wasn't. She was losing herself in anger. When she turned back to me, her voice was low but hard, 'Do you know that that could have killed him?'

I shook my head. I didn't know. I didn't know it could have happened just by leaving a toy in the basket with him.

Katherine stood up and walked away. She stopped by the desk for a moment, and she saw my secret chest. I hadn't shut it. She picked up the watch that had stopped the day before Alfie died. She looked as though she was about to speak, and then I watched her as she caught sight of something. She picked it up, and touched it, and looked thoughtful and confused.

Her voice was low as she said, 'What's this, Leila?'

'What?'

Katherine held her palm open and showed me what she'd found. It was the lock of Alfie's hair, lying unwrapped on a piece of tissue.

I shrugged. 'It's somebody's hair.'

'Whose hair? Do you know?'

'No.'

Katherine held it just beneath her nose and inhaled. 'Can I keep this?'

'Why?'

'Because I think it belongs to Alfie, and I want to know how you got it.'

I stayed silent, but she wouldn't go away. She said, 'Is this Alfie's hair?' and in the end I said, 'Yes.'

•

I didn't go to the funeral. I didn't want to see any more of that alien world where adults had lost control and vanished to a place they would never come back from. I built myself a den in my room. I had a piece of white mesh attached to a turret that hung from the ceiling. It draped over the floor like a tent. I could tie the doors back if I'd wanted, but I kept them shut. I thought no one would find me in there. After a few days, I spread cushions and a rug on the floor, and slept on them instead of in my bed.

Weeks passed. People stopped talking. Katherine didn't speak to my father, my father didn't speak to Katherine, and no one from outside spoke to either of them. Eventually, they decided to send me away for a weekend. It was Katherine's idea. She wanted to spend time with my father. She wanted them to reach out to each other, instead of drifting further and further apart. She wanted them to build something personal in Alfie's memory, something they could keep and look after.

They settled on a garden. A small memorial garden in the grounds of our bigger garden. They would fill it with roses and lilies. They'd string white lights in the trees and my father would make a bench, a wooden two-seater with a plaque: In memory of Alfie. Aged 37 days. Beloved.

As I left on Friday afternoon, he was already hacking at the fir trees.

•

They found the doll, of course. They found her in her grave, bald and full of mud, with a jagged cut, mended with old wet tape. It was Katherine who opened her again. She heard the rattle of something in the doll's body. She looked inside, and found Alfie's scan photo. It was wet and crumpled, but she knew it immediately.

When I came home, my father talked to me. He wanted to know why I'd done it. I couldn't answer. I didn't know myself.

I went upstairs. The door to my father's bedroom was open a little way. I stood in the splinter of light and looked in. Katherine was lying on her back on the bed. Her hand was clenched to a fist, and she was rubbing it against her chest, over and over to take the edge off the pain. Music was playing on the CD player in the corner. But it wasn't real music. It was the sound of water.

I watched her for a while. She carried on, rubbing her fist over her chest and breathing long, deep breaths. She wasn't crying. She was looking at the ceiling. Then she turned her head, and saw me standing at the door, and she said, 'Please go away and leave me alone.' I thought, *She's so sad; it's going to kill her.* Her voice when she'd spoken had been hardly more than a whisper. She needed all her energy just to lie there on the bed and be alive.

I turned away and walked up the stairs to my room. I crawled between the drapes of net that formed the front of my den, and tied them together with the cotton strings inside. Then I laid down on the cushions and curled my knees up to my chest, and put my hands together and started to pray.

•

Katherine went to the police and asked them to question me. I heard her tell my father it was what she was going to do. The doll in the garden and the lock of hair were minor. She was already suspicious. Alfie had been suffocated. She hadn't done it, my father hadn't done it, so it had to be me because, despite what everyone said, she knew it was no accident.

It was summer by then. June or July. They sent a woman to question me. I lied in all my answers–

'Did you see Alfie the night that he died?' – No.

'When was the last time you saw him?' – When my dad put him to bed.

'Did you like having a baby brother, Leila?' – He wasn't exactly my brother.

'Half-brother, then. Did you like having him around?' – Yes.

'Can you remember how you felt when they told you about him for the first time?' – Happy.

'Where did you get the lock of hair you kept in your secret chest?' – I found it.

'Where?' – On his pillow.

And so it went on.

She went next door afterwards, to speak to Rosie. Rosie didn't lie.

She came back and spoke to me. For a while – not long – Rosie became a serious suspect. A policeman came up from the station and joined in. Second opinion. They spoke to my father. They spoke to Alison.

We were just two ordinary little girls. That was their conclusion, eventually, once the loose ends were tied up. It was official. We were nothing to worry about.

•

It didn't stop Katherine, though. She was certain. 'I will keep trying,' she told my father. 'Unless you do something, I will keep on with this.'

She said other things, too: that I was disturbed; I was lonely; I was cruel and violent; I was secretive; I was beyond help; I was too much under Rosie's influence; Rosie was the real bully, I was the victim; I would be OK if I didn't see Rosie again, if I had a change of environment for a while…

I thought, *Not all those things can be true.*

Not at the same time, at least.

•

I never fully understood what happened next. The house was still thick with the madness of grief. I wondered whether my father had thought of leaving her. Maybe he didn't have the energy. Maybe he didn't want to. Maybe he thought it was best to stay with her. If he left her, she'd have pursued me.

Prospectuses started arriving on the doorstep. Every day, there was another one. Tall, imposing school buildings with towers and jagged edges. He went to look at some without me. He had long discussions with headmistresses about pastoral care and provision for emotional well-being. He inspected their meals. He wanted me well fed. He found out about sport and music and art and drama. He wanted martial arts, and lots of time for expression.

He found one in the end. Rotherfield Hall. I started there in September. I wasn't yet ten.

•

The first three years dragged. I never went home. Katherine wouldn't have me, and my father had his own agenda. He visited me on occasional weekends, and brought me sweets that I longed for but never ate. I hid them in a tin under my bed. I counted them every night before I went to sleep.

I did well at school. It surprised them. The staff saw me as troubled. My nightmares had come back, but this time they weren't about my mother. They were about Alfie. They wouldn't let me have a roommate. I'd only have upset her.

They didn't know what to do with me. Outside lessons, I did nothing but read. I wanted to be a girl in a book, and felt huge loss when I realised I never would be. I was quiet, but I caused no trouble. Other troubled girls made a fuss and were rude. I didn't. I didn't fit into any particular category.

•

I moved up to the senior school a year early. A pointless exercise, as far as I could see. It meant I'd be leaving a year earlier and the school would lose out on a set of fees. But that was probably why they'd done it – the money was a small price to pay to get rid of me.

For a long time, I was still convinced that my father would come and get me. He'd leave Katherine. He was only with her because he thought he had no choice.

He visited more often. I was twelve when he broke the news. 'Katherine's pregnant again.' I knew then I would never go home. I knew then that he must have loved her. It offended me, that he could be having sex while I was there, living among strangers, stuck in my miserable bedroom without even a roommate to share the bleakness with. It was bleak. The school would try and persuade us otherwise, but bleak was the only word for it.

•

They gave me a roommate eventually, but she left after a year to join her parents in Saudi Arabia. I spent the summer with my guardians just outside town. Guardians were there to put us up if we couldn't go home. They got good money for having us. Mine weren't strict, but they lived in the middle of nowhere, so there was still nothing to do. I started smoking that year, just before I turned fourteen. There was nothing else to spend my pocket money on. My father gave me money every week. A generous amount. I supposed it made him feel better.

•

In September, I went back to school and a girl I'd seen but never spoken to became my new roommate. She'd been at a school in Marlborough, but she'd come to Rotherfield Hall because of an abuse scandal in the boarding houses. Her parents lived in New York, so she, too, never went home. They thought we'd make a good pair. They thought we'd become friends. They thought a friend was what I needed.

'Leila, this is Olivia, your new roommate for this year. I'm sure you'll help her settle in.'

I looked at her. She smiled at me.

Later, I touched her, just to make sure she was there.

Part Three

I

In October, once Leila had gone up to Oxford, Gus would be leaving, too. It was a decision Katherine had reached with him. Quietly now, and without acrimony, they'd finally arrived at the destination they'd been moving towards – sometimes hurtling, sometimes crawling, but always on their way – for the last eight-and-a-half years.

Katherine would be keeping the house. She'd also have all three children during the week, and Isaac all the time until he was two. Until then, his father would have to make do with short visits when he picked the girls up, or dropped them off from their weekends with him. Aside from their relationship and the loving security Katherine had always wanted for her family, her loss was smaller. But there was fear: she was now facing life as the single mother of three young children, with hardly a career history and no money of her own, and the condition her doctor tactfully referred to as 'an understandable vulnerability to depression.'

Considering the amount of time they'd spent reaching this point, she was thinking now that they could have planned it better. Only Grace was at school full-time. Lily and Isaac would need to be put into nursery, or they'd need a nanny while she worked. The thought of it made her recoil. It was something she'd never wanted for her children, but they had so much now that she'd never wanted for them, and she didn't see herself as having any other choice. Although in theory the maintenance Gus was willing to pay would be enough to keep them all, she couldn't justify her own living from funds meant for them. She also wasn't sure her pride would handle it, though that was a secondary concern – she could quash her desire for independence if it was what the children needed. But she also knew that she would flounder, staying here alone with three young children and the memory of one more, isolated, barely seeing another adult. The world would turn. It would suck her in, take her down.

At the moment, she was doing well. Once, only once since they'd decided to separate had she given in and cried – to top it off, still post-natal and hormonal. This, she thought – that she was facing, that she had already faced – was not the life she'd planned for herself. When she was younger, still struggling with the decision about what to do with her life, and still sufficiently deluded to think that such a decision existed and that no outside force could ever alter it once made, she'd written optimistic, goal-focussed lists: Things to do Before Twenty-Five, Things to do Before Thirty (forty was overlooked, being too far away), Things to do This Year. Essentially, they'd always amounted to the same thing: Don't be Ordinary. Have Substance. Achieve.

In her mind, she'd allowed for tragedy. She'd allowed for tragedy on a normal, everyday scale. She believed in sadness and grief, and what it did to people – forced them to realise their limits, their vulnerability, their capacity for devastation. She liked to think that, once the rawness had healed, sorrow would breed compassion, and as far as she could see, compassion was humanity's only hope.

But she hadn't allowed for this. She hadn't allowed for loss on this scale, and all its terrifying sadness. She hadn't imagined anger this overwhelming. She was consumed, even now, with what felt like a deeply primitive urge for vengeance. It shocked her. If she were honest – truly, darkly honest – she knew that what she wanted, more than anything else, was to see Leila suffer and suffer and suffer, and then die. And seeing it was key. It wouldn't be enough just to be told it was happening. She wanted her fistful of blood. She wanted to take that pretty red heart in both her hands and wring it.

She was resigned to the fact now that vengeance, or even justice – if there could be any justice for the life of her child – would probably never be hers. Leila would go on living, charming people, pushing away guilt. But still, Katherine thought, she was able to take a satisfied comfort from the fact that, in that sense, she was doing well out of the separation. Without even meaning to, she'd managed to secure Leila's inheritance away from her. Ash Farm now belonged to Grace, Lily and Isaac. It was no longer hers, and never would be again.

•

For years, Katherine had hardly spoken about Leila, though together with Alfie, for a long time the girl had dominated her thoughts. In her desperation to feel some sense of justice, she'd always been preoccupied with Leila's pain. Did she have any? Was the guilt destroying her as it should be? Or did she, like a genuine psychopath, find ways of validating her actions and blaming someone else? Leila's guilt was crucial to Katherine. She was never going to be punished in any other way. Her father would make sure of that, always.

Now, no one knew how Leila still consumed her. It was rage she had to control. Everyone, almost without exception, thought she had moved on, in the civilised way that people were supposed to move on: to keep marching forwards through time. They didn't know that time itself was the killer. It didn't heal and bring relief. It made everything worse. Eight years without their child had been bleaker and more painful than one year. Gus had another thirty to go. She had more.

Three years after losing Alfie, late into her pregnancy with Grace, she thought she was ill, and possibly also that she'd lost her mind. Grief still overwhelmed her. It attacked her unexpectedly – in supermarkets when she saw parents with their sons, or grandparents with grandsons, sometimes while simply planting bulbs in the garden – and put her in bed for days. There were times when the pain of losing him could feel as violent as the pain of giving birth to him, except worse, because he wouldn't be arriving at the end of it. She knew, because she'd searched. Everywhere she went, she looked for him. She'd hunted for his handprints on the side of the baby bath, scrutinised his toys for white crusts of dribble. There were times when she questioned whether she'd always been fated to lose him – her grief had begun almost from the moment he was born. For three days afterwards, she'd still been able to feel him inside her. He'd elbowed the empty folds of her belly. She'd woken to a kick that wasn't there. If they cut her open, the doctors would have found him. They'd have seen his shadow on her womb, found traces of his blood or skin.

What had worried her most back then was that she wouldn't welcome her second baby. She wouldn't forgive Grace for not being Alfie, so in the end, without telling Gus, she found herself a bereavement therapist. Every Wednesday morning for the next year and a half, she paid fifty pounds to sit on a sofa in his front room for an hour, amidst wooden shelves lined with heavy textbooks: *Guiding the Bereaved*, *The Stages of Grief*, *Children: The Forgotten Mourners*.

He spoke to her gently. 'What precipitated your decision to come here?'

She had no words to dilute it by then. She said the only thing she could, pushing her voice into the cool world of the clinician. 'My baby died three years ago. He was five weeks old. I think he was killed by my partner's child, but no one will listen to me. I can't stop thinking about it. I think I might be insane.'

He looked at her and nodded. He asked calm questions about the death, the inquest, the impact on the family. He let her overrun, and talk into the next hour without extra charge. Finally, he said, 'What is it that makes you think your partner's daughter killed him?'

She floundered again, as she always did. 'Leila was a troubled child. When she was five, she was involved in a car crash that killed her mother. The loss of his wife hit my partner very hard, and I know he neglected Leila in the months afterwards, and probably again when he met me. But it was more than that. I know most children would have been troubled by those circumstances, but Leila…'

He asked the question again. 'What makes you think she killed him?'

'I am certain that she killed him.'

He didn't ask another time. He simply looked at her in the interested, slightly patronising way that professional people dealt with the highly distressed, and expected her to continue.

Eventually, she stumbled through it, listing reason after reason, each one weak by itself. Nothing she said was based in hard, physical evidence. It was physical evidence the police had wanted, and there were only two pieces, and neither of them strong enough.

On the night of his death, Katherine had put Alfie to sleep in his moses basket in the nursery, instead of in their bedroom. (They'd been trying to re-activate their sex life, another thing she had now never forgiven herself for.) He didn't have a blanket, or a toy, or anything that could have harmed him. He slept fastened into his sleeping bag. In the morning, she went to get him, and he was dead. The post-mortem revealed bruising from suffocation, but she had put nothing – nothing – in the basket that could have suffocated a baby.

The monitor had been tampered with. It was damaged. (She put that down to Rosie.)

'And I could go on,' she said in the end. 'I could go on listing more and more reasons, but the fact is, I know. I just know.'

In eighteen months, the therapist never said whether he agreed or disagreed. She suspected that he, too, might privately think she was mad.

'My job isn't to apply blame to his death,' he said. 'What happened in the past can't be changed. What matters is now, and finding ways to help you cope with it.'

At that point, it felt like a waste of money. Katherine was paying him – or, rather ironically, Gus was paying him, as it was he who earned all the money in their joint account, and she'd told him about it eventually – to take her side and believe her. The question mark over Alfie's death hadn't taken her there. What had taken her was the fact that she wanted to be a good mother to her future children, and she wasn't sure she could be for as long as she felt this angry. As well as that, she was terrified that this one would die, too. After Alfie, she'd thought she was protected. Pain itself was protective – once you crossed a threshold, you could never be any more hurt. But it wasn't true. Life didn't work in some neat, kind way. There was no compassionate higher power, looking down benevolently and saying, 'She's had enough to deal with. I'll be kinder to her now, and batter someone else with grief.' No. She could always lose another one. And another one.

'If Leila killed your baby,' the therapist asked once, 'do you think you are wrong to feel this way? Aside from the fact that forgiveness can often help heal a victim, do you think you should forgive her?'

'No.'

'Of course, this is complicated by the fact that she is your partner's child, but would it ever occur to you that you might forgive a stranger who'd done the same thing?'

'No.'

And that was what she spent nearly two thousand pounds coming to accept.

She would never recover from losing her child. She did not need to forgive that which would always be unforgivable.

•

They hadn't told Grace yet that her father would be moving out in less than four weeks. There was nothing to say to Lily or Isaac. She wondered how they would process the loss. Perhaps they'd be dimly aware of his absence for a while, then carry on growing up, unaffected by it. But that, she knew, was wishful thinking. Her own parents were divorced, and Katherine had spent her childhood craving the monthly weekends with her father, and then mourning them before they were even over. After the excitement of Friday night and Saturdays full of swimming and ice skating and her father's loving presence, she'd wake up on Sunday mornings deflated and depressed, knowing that once today was over, there'd be another three weeks of life to get through with her stressed, short-tempered, and harshly disciplinarian mother before it all came round again.

It was autumn, and Grace was back at school now. Isaac was sleeping. Katherine had a copy of the local newspaper, spread out over the kitchen table, open at the Classifieds section, and was circling adverts for work she could combine with singled parenthood. When she was twenty-six, she'd qualified as a primary school teacher, but then she'd met Gus, fallen pregnant with Alfie, and never completed her probationary year, so full-time teaching work would be difficult to find. It was what would suit her best, despite the low salary. She knew she would never again have the lifestyle Gus's salary had provided. It didn't bother her.

Beside her, Lily marched determinedly up and down the kitchen with her toy pushchair, containing a naked, upside-down doll, which she stooped now and then to feed from her plastic dish of carrot sticks. 'Eat it,' she ordered, in her high-pitched baby voice. It was her newest phrase.

Katherine smiled at her. She tried not to think too much as she drew a neat blue ring around the phone number for an agency placing supply teachers. In her maternal vision of herself, which was – sadly perhaps, in these modern times – the only real vision of herself she'd ever constructed, she'd always planned to stay at home until her youngest reached five, steadfast in her belief that the most precious thing she could give them was her time. There would be no nannies, no au pairs, no part-time help they could haul in from Eastern Europe and pay a pittance to drudge through work they were capable of doing themselves. She was to be a baker of bread, a teller of stories, a mother of infinite patience. She would never be bored, or short-tempered, or upset, or long for a more intellectually fulfilling life. She would embrace her tiny world, drunk on the immensity of what they'd created.

There were moments, over the last five years, when she'd achieved all of this, though they were rare and fleeting.

Isaac sighed and whimpered through the baby monitor. She looked at the clock. Gus and Leila were out again, driving. It seemed to be the only thing he could do now to get her out of bed, the only structure she had to her days, apart from ploughing through endless volumes of Victorian literature in preparation for going up to Oxford. She didn't appear to be doing much of that, though. She didn't appear to be doing anything, except wandering now and then, Lady Macbeth-like, from room to room. Katherine wondered whether this apparent depression was a show for her father's sake, or a real, genuine point of breakdown. Perhaps she'd had a revelation, a moment when she realised the enormity of what she'd done, and the fact that the consequences would keep rolling on and on forever, not growing smaller with time, but bigger.

She tore the teaching agency's advert out of the paper and pinned it to the board on the wall above the phone. She'd ring them later.

She turned to Lily, who was trying to yank the wheels of her pushchair from where it had become stuck between a cupboard and a chair leg. 'Are you ready for some lunch?'

Lily turned her head and looked at her in desperation. Katherine went over to her, and pulled the pushchair neatly away. 'There,' she said, and all of a sudden it seemed impossible that she was about to allow somebody else to perform these intimate acts of rescue for her child. They were hers. She wasn't ready to let them go, or even share them.

'Lunch?' she asked again.

Lily nodded. 'Lunch.'

She began slicing bread and cutting fruit and cheese and arranging them on a plastic plate. The kitchen door opened behind her and she looked round. It was Olivia.

'Hi, Liv. Are you hungry?'

Olivia shook her head. 'I'm fine.' She sat down on the floor and started talking to Lily.

'Leila and Gus are out.'

'I know.'

'But they'll be back soon, I'm sure.'

Olivia shrugged. 'It's OK. I don't mind.'

She sensed that Olivia was fed up, and possibly that she wanted to talk to her.

She carried Lily's plate to the table.

Olivia lifted Lily off the floor and strapped her into her booster seat. Katherine had seen that the children charmed her. It made her easier to like, though in fact, liking her hadn't been hard. The letter from their housemistress had frightened Katherine because of its focus on two obsessive girls, and she'd seen enough of that eight years ago between Leila and Rosie. But Olivia was fine. She was also, quite clearly, utterly besotted with Leila. A well-worn blueprint for disaster.

They took seats at the table – Katherine beside Lily and Olivia opposite. Olivia was pretty, in the way that most privileged young people were pretty: fresh-faced, healthy, and radiating confidence in their certainty that, for the rest of their lives, the world would continue to be as exciting and kind to them as it had been until now. She was eighteen and still optimistic. Two weeks ago, they'd gone back to Rotherfield Hall to collect their exam results. Both of them had done impressively well, and of course Leila had secured her place on the school's Board of Honour, hung up in the entrance hall, large enough to be unmissable: *Name: Leila Hartley, Destination: The Queen's College, Oxford.*

Olivia looked uneasy. She linked her fingers together and bent her hands until her knuckles cracked. Katherine made it easier for her. 'Are you all right?'

She smiled politely and delivered what sounded like rehearsed words. 'Thank you for putting me up this summer, Katherine, but I've been thinking I might go home and spend the last few weeks of the holiday with my family.'

Katherine said, 'Are you sure? You know you don't have to.' She paused, imagining Leila here on her own without her girlfriend to keep her away from the family. The thought made her anxious. 'I'm sure Leila would miss you.'

Olivia nodded. 'I know. But I don't think she's very well, and there's nothing I can do.'

Just then, Isaac woke up and started to cry. 'Hold on one moment,' Katherine said, standing up to go and get him. She touched Olivia lightly on the shoulder as she passed.

Upstairs, she picked up the baby and changed him. He wailed. She made soothing, understanding noises. He was almost exactly the same age Alfie had been when he died. When it was over, she swaddled him in a yellow shawl and carried him downstairs. (Unfashionable though it was, she believed in swaddling, tightly packing babies into environments where they were held fast like muscle.)

'Sorry,' she said, walking back down to the kitchen. She sat at the table and latched the baby onto her breast. He stopped crying and sucked greedily.

Olivia smiled. Katherine said, 'You were telling me about Leila.'

'It's all right. It doesn't matter.'

Katherine wanted to push it. She wanted to find out, as far as she could, what went on in Leila's head. She was going to drive this now until she knew about guilt.

She said, 'Do you think she's unhappy here?'

'I don't know. I think she's unhappy everywhere.'

This was news she'd never heard before. She'd always pictured Leila, out in her protected world, smiling, successful, happy, simply nursing a secret she tried never to think about. It was only Katherine and her father who had to battle on together with their loss. Gus would go through anything for Leila, do anything to keep her safe, to spare her from witnessing the impact of what she'd done. That was the real reason he hadn't fought to bring her home in earlier years.

Katherine spoke evenly, and stroked Isaac's hair as he fed. 'I'm sorry for her, if that's true.'

Olivia sounded surprised. 'Oh, it is true. Of course.'

'Of course?'

'Well…'

She looked uncomfortable. Katherine said, 'It's all right. I can talk about the baby we lost, if you think that's what's troubling Leila.'

Olivia smiled, though she said nothing.

'You and Leila seem to be very close.'

'We are.'

In all the time they'd been here, neither Katherine nor Gus had let on that they knew about the girls' relationship. The girls worked hard to hide it, but Katherine had seen them hand in hand in the garden, stealing kisses when they thought no one could see. She had also, once or twice when they'd first arrived, overheard their breathlessness, the excitement, the energetic squeaking of springs.

Katherine asked, 'What do you think is wrong with her?'

'I don't know.'

She looked down at Isaac. His eyes were closed but his lips still moved furiously. 'Do you think it's being here?'

'Probably. I think she's finding it hard…to move on.'

'That's something all of us find hard.'

'I hope you don't mind. Her father told her he'd be moving out soon, and I think she feels it's her fault in some way. For being here.'

'That really should be the least of her worries.'

There was an edge to her voice that she hadn't intended. Olivia looked startled.

Katherine smiled again. 'I'm sorry. I didn't mean to sound quite so ferocious.'

'It's OK.'

She spoke carefully. 'Has Leila ever told you why we sent her away to school?'

Olivia stared at the table. She nodded. Lily laughed from her booster seat, holding out hands that were sticky with butter and tomato pips. Katherine reached for a tissue and wiped them. Lily leant forwards and looked at Isaac. She pointed a finger. 'Baby,' she whispered.

They sat for a while in silence, then Katherine said, 'There's a lot that Leila and her father need to resolve, and they can't do it here, where I am and where the children are. I think that's one thing we all agree on.'

'No. I understand that.'

She looked sad. Katherine had an uncertain impulse to embrace her. The girl was out of her depth. It was impossible for her to make sense of something this messy, and venomous. She asked, 'What was Leila like at school?'

Olivia tumbled out mouthfuls of adoring adjectives. Katherine listened. 'You don't believe Leila would hurt anyone.'

'No. No, I can't believe it. It's impossible for me. I think,' she paused and looked away, taking care with words, 'I think that's what's making her so unhappy. Knowing what you think of her, and not knowing how she can change your mind.'

'She wants me to change my mind.' (Her months of therapy had taught Katherine the technique of gently stating the obvious during moments of potential conflict.)

'Of course she would.'

'Do you really think she's ill?'

'Yes.'

Katherine nodded, and took it in. She wanted to put it down to remorse, Leila's rapid descent into wretchedness, and she wanted her to stay there. Wild justice.

She said, 'Has Leila ever told you what her father thinks about Alfie's death?'

'Not really. She doesn't talk about it very much.'

For a moment, Katherine hesitated. Then she said, 'He thinks she did it. He thinks she killed our son, and that's why he kept her at school.'

She had to turn away from the look on Olivia's face. Silently, she asked herself, *What are you doing?* Her words would not disappear now. They were there in the air between them, as clearly as if she'd written them. She pushed her thoughts away. She didn't want to examine the reasons behind this – this desire to inflict pain on the girl whose only crime was to love Leila. It was Leila she wanted to hurt, not Olivia. That, Katherine knew, was why she was doing it. She wanted to break them apart. Leila had no right to a love like this.

II

Olivia

At last, the summer's heat was dying. Days and nights were becoming bearable again, the sun lost its glare and dusk fell earlier. In the new cool of the evenings, the garden became my refuge.

I made my escape from the house and sat on the ground under the shade of a copper beech. On the grass by the swimming pool, a peacock paraded before its mate. I didn't understand keeping peacocks the way normal people kept budgies in cages. It was bordering on the pretentious. They were also very noisy.

The sun behind me slipped slowly down to the hills. A silent plane zipped open the sky, and all around me, bees droned among the last of the flowers.

For days now, Leila had barely spoken to me. She'd barely crawled out of bed. She was miserable. When we were at school, she used to say she didn't mind being sad – it was more interesting than every day, uncomplicated happiness. This was different. Leila was gone. When I spoke to her, or tried to touch her, she wasn't there.

My thoughts now were turning to my own survival. I couldn't stay here much longer, in this house where every room was taut with misery and hostility that had nothing to do with me. Almost since the day we'd arrived, Gus and Katherine had argued, and last week they announced that they were separating. Yesterday, I phoned my mother and asked if I could stay with them in Manhattan for the last few weeks of the holidays. She said yes. In fact, she sounded pleased. She said she'd get my father to book me a flight. She didn't ask if anything was wrong, which was a relief. My decision wasn't born out of choice. As far as I could see, there was nothing else I could do, and this struck me as being the only way Leila and I could survive into the future. I was nervous. I had no faith anymore in my ability to get by without her. Or perhaps I'd get by, but I'd never get used to it.

In the garden next door, I could hear Rosie and her mother talking in low, serious voices. I'd met her mother twice, and this afternoon I ran into her at the post office when I was buying Air Mail stamps for the States. She looked at me curiously and, like Rosie a few weeks ago, asked how I was finding it here. There'd been a secretiveness to her tone that made me wary, though I was growing desperate for someone to confide in. I shrugged and said, 'Not too bad, which I hoped was a suitably ambiguous response, despite the fact that I was tired of ambiguity and uncertainty. I wanted something solid, something definite to hold on to.

All I was certain of now was that I couldn't bear Rosie. Recently, Leila said she thought she'd changed, but I didn't believe it. All I could see was someone jealous and manipulative, with no grasp of other people's feelings. I hadn't told Leila I didn't like her, or mentioned the kiss she pressed on me. I didn't dare. Somewhere, I questioned now where Leila's loyalty lay, and I wasn't ready to face it yet if it wasn't with me.

There were two reasons I could think of to explain Leila's sadness. The first was delayed grief for her family. The second, of course, was guilt. But, no matter what Katherine said to me, I wouldn't make myself believe in her guilt. I couldn't. If I did, it would make her a different person – vicious, secretive, a hypocrite. In every way, she'd be the opposite of the person I knew, and I'd have to stop loving her, and that would be impossible. She was my rock, my earth, my day and night. She was all I had, and all I wanted to have.

I looked up and saw her coming across the garden. Her hair was hanging loose for once, the way she'd always worn it in school because they always told her not to. I liked it that way. She was wearing a pale pink dress that barely veiled her skin. I smiled at her. Her face was bare of make-up, white as shell.

She sat on the grass beside me and leant forwards and kissed me warmly on the lips. 'Rosie's coming over,' she said.

'Right,' I said. Then, without thinking, I added, 'Is that why you've managed to get out of bed today?'

She turned her head away from me. 'Liv, I…'

The silence that fell was frosty. I thought, *How did we get to this, barely able to speak to each other, when two months ago we were passionate and zealously adoring?* The suddenness was intolerable. It made it impossible to understand.

She raised her eyes to meet with mine. 'I didn't know it was going to be like this.'

There was nothing for me to say. Katherine's words from earlier kept bombarding my head. *He thinks she killed our son*. I was angry. I was furious with her for telling me. I was too young to deal with the confidences of a middle-aged woman, especially this one.

The dusk was turning slowly to night. A crescent moon had appeared in the sky above the house. The pool rippled with insects and the hoarse cries of baby frogs.

Leila leaned her head against my shoulder. For a moment, it was the closest we'd been since before Isaac was born.

She sat up abruptly. I looked where she was looking and saw Rosie. She had one leg planted on either side of the fence that split the two gardens. 'Hi,' she called, as though it were a ten-syllable word. She swung herself over the fence and manoeuvred neatly onto the grass.

Leila called, 'Hi.'

I ignored her.

She walked towards us, sat down, and lit a cigarette. It was her usual routine, another one Leila said she'd started at the age of ten.

'I'm sorry about your father and Katherine splitting up.'

'Who told you?' Leila asked.

'Katherine, of course. She and Alison speak again these days.'

'Of course,' Leila said. 'Sorry.' She reached over and helped herself to one of Rosie's cigarettes.

'It must be really tense.' Her tone now was sympathetic. She sounded at least moderately genuine.

'It is. It's awful.'

Rosie nodded. 'I'm sorry,' she said. Then she turned to me. 'No wonder you want to leave.'

Leila spun her head around to me. 'What?' she demanded.

'It's all right. Nothing's definite. It's just something I spoke about to Katherine earlier.'

Rosie's gaze shifted. 'Have I said the wrong thing?'

'Yes,' I snapped. 'Yes, you have actually, Rosie. It seems to be a habit of yours.'

'I didn't mean…'

'Of course not.'

Leila put her hand on my arm. 'Olivia…'

I shook her away and stood up. My voice was louder than I'd heard it for ages. 'I'm tired of this. I'm tired of her coming round, casually dropping bombshells, and then running away.' I turned back to Rosie. 'There's enough going on here without that.' My temper was taking even me by surprise. I lowered my voice and murmured to Leila, 'I'll see you later. I'm going inside.'

I strode back to the house. As usual, Katherine was in the kitchen. She looked up as I went in. 'What's wrong?'

'Nothing. I'm just so angry with Rosie.' *And you,* I thought. *And you.*

'Are you all right?'

'Yes.'

'I'm sorry this hasn't been a very good visit for you, Olivia.'

'Don't worry about it,' I said. The house was full of people's apologies. They were as exhausting as the events that created them.

I looked out of the window to where Leila and Rosie still sat in the garden. They were talking seriously, and then Rosie reached out her hand and ran it softly down Leila's cheek.

•

I went upstairs and started packing to go back to Manhattan. I wanted to be ready to go as soon as they gave me the word. I despised everyone here, not just Rosie. They were all mad, and living together, in this house, under one roof, made them all worse. There was only one person I was still prepared to listen to, but even she was distant and remote. I wanted to get away from her for a while as well.

I remembered Manhattan and my parents' apartment on the Upper West Side. My mother would take me shopping as soon as I arrived. She'd do what she always did, which was to gaze at me critically, re-arrange my hair, and then cast me a look of surrender, as though my appearance truly warranted her lack of tact. 'What happened to make-up, Olivia? Those clothes look like you picked them up in a rummage sale. I can see we'll really have to do some work on this before you leave.' I couldn't explain to her that Eastbourne was not like New York.

By now I was looking forward to a few weeks in the city. The entire world had closed in on me here. I wanted to walk down streets chock-full of people, to buy giant pretzels from a stall, to feel small among buildings, listen to the sound of pressure all around me that wasn't always being contained.

I piled everything in my suitcase and left it propped open against the wall. I reached under the bed and brought out the cast of Alfie's footprints. I still hadn't told anyone I'd broken it. I thought of leaving it there for someone else to find after I'd gone, or to wrap the pieces in newspaper and stuff them at the bottom of the bin outside. It was awful to be reckless with something that meant so much to them, but I couldn't face a confession. Besides that, I knew they'd never suspect me. It was Leila they would blame, and I doubted whether Leila would ever come home again. I put the cast down on the bed.

'What are you doing?'

I turned around and saw her there, standing in the doorway.

I said, 'I'm packing.'

'You're leaving.' Her words were flat. She wasn't going to argue. I doubted whether she had the strength for it.

'Not forever.'

Relief broke over her face like water. 'Are you sure?'

'Yes.'

She stood near me, but didn't look at me. 'I'm sorry it's been so awful for you. I'll be better soon, once we leave here, once term starts.'

'I wish you'd talk…'

She put her finger to my lips to silence me. She kissed me hard on the mouth. I responded. She pulled away.

'What is it?' I heard the impatience in my voice.

'Nothing. Sorry.'

I carried on packing.

She said, 'When are you going?'

'I don't know yet. My dad's booking me a flight.'

'Do you have to go?'

'Yes.'

'Can I talk you into staying?'

'Probably not.'

She sighed. 'OK.'

I turned and faced her. 'It's not that I want to go. I don't want to leave you. At all. But I can't handle it here anymore. It's so bloody claustrophobic. Everyone hates everyone else. Your dad's leaving, you've barely spoken to me for days, and I'm stuck in this house with people I hardly know, who are all miserable. And Rosie's here all the time, and she's the only person you seem interested in talking to.'

'You hate her.'

'I'm suspicious of her.'

'Why?'

'She's foul.'

'She's not that bad. Not really. Not once you get to know her.'

'Are you in love with her?'

'With Rosie?'

'Yes.'

'No. Not in the least.'

'Good.'

'Why are you asking me this?'

'I was just wondering. You've seemed very tight recently.'

'Listen, it's not…' She caught sight of the plaster cast on the bed. 'What's that?'

'It was under the bed when we got here. I broke it.'

She stared at it.

I said, 'It was an accident. I haven't told anyone yet.'

Long moments passed.

She moved towards the bed and took each piece in her hands. Her eyes filled with tears that didn't fall. I heard her swallow. Hard.

She looked around the room, then she said, 'This was his nursery.'

I said, 'You've told me that before.'

'It's where he slept when they didn't want him in their room. It's where he died.'

I'd guessed that, though I'd never been sure.

She kept on staring at the footprints in her hands. Her voice when she spoke again was barely more than a whisper. I had to lean forwards to catch it. She said, 'It's where I killed him.'

'What?'

She nodded. 'Yes.'

My first thought was that I couldn't see her face properly, and if I could, I'd know she was lying, or joking. She stood tense and rigid, with her shoulders hunched. I felt nauseous as I looked at her.

Eventually, she spoke again, still without looking at me. 'Say something.'

So I said, 'Are you sure?'

She was shaking her head. 'Don't make me say it again.' There was desperation in her voice. I'd never heard it there before.

In the room next to us, Isaac started crying. Almost immediately came the sound of Katherine's footfall on the stairs below. When I'd seen her with her children, I'd wondered sometimes whether I'd ever been adored with such endless, mindless devotion. It seemed unlikely. My own mother wasn't the type to become besotted by a baby, a being who was just a helpless string of emotions arranged around a gut. I listened to Katherine's voice as she soothed him. Her tenderness hurt.

I sat down on the bed. Leila stood opposite me. I looked at her, her pale face and her blonde hair, her pretty wet lips that had touched every part of my body, and I thought, *My beautiful girl is a murderer.*

But it was impossible. It was as impossible as it had always been.

I said, 'Leila, are you lying?'

'Please don't do this.'

Katherine took the baby downstairs. He was still crying.

Leila said, 'I don't know what to do.'

'Neither do I.'

Silence fell between us again. It wasn't icy this time. It was furious and heavy. My thoughts hit me relentlessly, shocked and unformed. I didn't hear them in my head like language. I felt them at the pit of my stomach like sickness, but I knew, however unreal they still were, what they would mean tomorrow, or the next day, once the shock had stopped protecting me from them. *I have been deluded, and I was a fool, and she was cruel.*

The betrayal was huge.

I had no idea how to reach her. I wasn't sure I still wanted to reach her. The Leila I knew had crumbled away like rock, and in her place stood a stranger, a criminal, the worst of criminals.

I should hate her, I thought. I'd always thought she'd suffered, but suddenly I realised: *She has not been hurt like they have.*

I said, 'How have you lived with this?'

She didn't answer. I said it again, more urgently. 'How have you lived with this?'

'I don't know.'

For all your supposed intelligence, I thought, *you don't even know how you live from day to day.*

I said, 'You must know. For nearly nine years you have lived every single day knowing you killed a child, your father's child, Katherine's child…'

She looked genuinely terrified. 'Please keep your voice down.'

'They already know, Leila. It was me who thought it couldn't possibly be you. I thought it had to be Rosie, if it was anyone at all.'

She turned away from me. 'It wasn't Rosie.'

'Was she there? Did she…'

'No. Rosie didn't do anything.'

'But was she there?'

She still wouldn't turn around. She carried on talking, 'She was there that night, but only I was there when he died. She didn't know.' She walked over to the mantelpiece, where she stood the broken plaster cast against the wall, the pieces slotted neatly together. On the wall in front of her were the photographs of Alfie, protected in their glass frames.'

I said, 'Does Rosie know now?'

She kept her back towards me. 'She knew the next day. She knew, and never told anyone.'

I spoke slowly, 'So all this time, it was nothing to do with Rosie. It was just you.'

'It wasn't…'

'And for years, you've had me convinced that Katherine was cruel to send you away, and yet you killed her baby.' My mind reeled. I'd spent the summer trying not to like Katherine too much, never being too warm towards her out of my misplaced loyalty to Leila. I felt awful, as though I, too, had now inflicted even more pain on her.

'Listen. It's complicated.'

'I am listening. I have always taken your side. Always. I want to know why you've always been so nasty about Katherine.' I thought, *Is it because you are simply a nasty, horrible person, who has tricked me for all this time?*

She turned round to face me at last, and sighed. 'Because it was easier. I don't know what you do with a guilt like this, other than push it away and blame someone else when you're forced to think of it. If I could convince myself that it was her fault…'

'You could never have done that.'

'Not really. But I tried.'

I stopped talking and tried to take it all in. I shook my head. 'How can you say all this so calmly?'

'How do you want me to say it? Do you want me to weep blood?'

The expression on her face was heartbreaking. I said nothing. I thought, *Yes. Yes, weep blood. Weep blood and let me forgive you.*

'Because I do.'

'OK.'

'Every minute.'

I said, 'What are you going to do?'

She stared at me, dumbly. 'Do?'

'Do you think you should do something? Say something to Katherine?'

'I can't. I can never do that.'

'I think you should.'

She paused. 'What can I say?'

I was stuck there, too. What could she say? There was nothing. *Sorry* was hardly sufficient.

'I have thought about it,' she said. 'And I don't think I should take my place at Oxford. Maybe I can try and make up for what I did in some other way. I mean, I know I can never make up for it, but perhaps I can do something, give something to someone else…I don't know…' She broke off, and looked embarrassed.

'What do you mean?'

'There are overseas programs. You can do voluntary work, develop skills that can help people, really get down to the bad stuff, the stuff no one wants to see…I can do that.' She shrugged. *Give life somewhere else*, was her feeble finish.

I nodded. It seemed like a good idea, in many ways. At least, it kept her human, and I needed that to hold on to. I said, 'I won't be able to be with you.'

She misunderstood me. I meant I couldn't be with her if she went abroad. Because despite everything, I still wanted her now.

For the first time since she'd told me, I raised my head and looked at her. She came and sat beside me again, and looked back at me. Her eyes met mine. My reflection appeared in her pupil, reduced, but still there, in every minute detail.

I put my arms around her. Things had changed, probably forever, but she was still Leila. She was still the same girl I adored, and could never stop adoring.

'I love you,' I told her.

I said it because I felt it. I always felt it. That was the trouble.

III

Leila

But if this cursed hand were thicker than itself with brother's blood, is there not rain enough in the sweet heavens to wash it white as snow?

Those weren't my words, of course. I'd had to read them in our English class at school. Hamlet. I took the part of the evil king. My teacher was so impressed with the authenticity of my guilt, she'd predicted me a future with the RSC.

I knew joking was poor taste. There was nothing funny about any of this. The ripples of death spread far and wide, but I was flailing among them just like everyone else was, and there was nothing I could do to make it better. Nothing.

But I would have done it, if I could. I'd have sacrificed anything for the chance to reach back through time, un-smother him and blow his breath back. I hadn't known, that night, as I sat upstairs and listened to the breath go, that it would be gone forever.

The truth?

That was the truth. *I hadn't known.*

No warden in any jail would ever have believed me. After all, I'd had early exposure to death, and as far as they could tell, I'd not seen my mother rise from her grave in the years since she'd been gone.

But it was true. I'd thought I was doing my mother a favour. Sending her a family. A baby is a baby. I couldn't tell the difference between hers and Katherine's. And when I could, it was too late. He was dead and everyone was miserable, and I was responsible, and it was permanent and irreversible. Bald facts. I couldn't change them.

It took years, that one. Accepting I couldn't change them. Time is cruel. A relentless one-way street to the end of the world. It would be easier if life, like botched knitting, could be undone.

At school, they caught me creeping into the chapel late at night. I did it often. I tried bartering with God, who they'd told me was all-powerful. If you give Alfie back, God, I'll believe in you for the rest of my life. That was my starter. It didn't work. I moved on.

Please God, why not take pity on them and send him back? They don't deserve this. I'll do a swap. You can have me instead if you want. I'll do it painfully if that would help. How do you want my body? Cut, starved, burned? I can do whatever you want. It's your choice. I can break my neck on a noose if that's how you want it.

I stopped that eventually, after a few years. I stopped just before Olivia came. I could see, in my ever-the-shining-schoolgirl way, that it was helping no one. I reined in the self-destruction. I carried it on a leash. I took me to the edge of death, but I always flipped me back.

I found other ways of living, that weren't real. I didn't trust myself around real people. They'd hurt me, or I'd hurt them. I didn't care about me – self-destruction is at heart altruistic. I cared what I'd do to others. I'd already proved that I was murderous.

I consumed books instead. I fell in love with the men and women inside them. My fictional passion knew no bounds. I was the tenderest and most desirous of lovers. The end of a novel left me bereft. I wrote my own sequels.

After Olivia came, I felt better. She saved me; she was real. From the start, I wanted to tell her. I built up to it, bit by bit: I never go home, because my father's *partner hates me. Her baby died and she thinks it was me who killed him.*

Always, I shied away at the last moment. She'd despise me, and I couldn't do without her. We lived like a pair of parasites, she and I, each clinging to the other for survival. We did it for years, but the neediness didn't negate the love, despite what pseudo-psychologists said. The love was real. It was the truest thing I'd ever encountered, though it, too, began as an illusion.

At fourteen, in our room at night, we used to act out scenes from *Romeo and Juliet*. We worked in secret, murmuring voices. That was how it all started. They thought we were devoted to literature, but it was each other we truly desired. We masked our feelings in fiction, until the boundaries blurred and it all became real.

It was easier, then, not to think. It was easier to simply lie back with her and find memory utterly empty.

It was the bloody, blood-red coming home that filled it up again.

What right did I have to Olivia, when Katherine and my father were still barely sewn up? I knew it was Katherine's doing – putting her in the room that used to be Alfie's. She was deliberately applying the guilt, pouring it over me and hoping I'd drown in it. She wanted to watch me crack open and repent. Steadfastly, I refused. I would hold on to my integrity. Oh, I could slice my heart out and serve it to her on a silver platter if she'd wanted it, but it would still have left her without her child. Nothing would ever be enough.

So I did nothing.

•

Rosie knew. Rosie always knew.

He was still alive that night when we took him up to my room. Alive, breathing, unharmed. Rosie said she'd hurt him. Sometimes I thought she was all bravado. I showed no bravado at all, but I wanted him dead just as much as she did. Once it had started, I couldn't stop wanting it, knowing as he struggled and coughed that he was breathing his last. It was heady and exciting. In law, they called it Irresistible Impulse. A defence. *Not guilty by reason of insanity.*

I regretted it. Immediately, I regretted it. The purple face and the stillness. I lay in bed, thinking about it, and then I raced back down the stairs, picked him up again and shook him. He didn't move. Not one loll of his big baby head.

I thought, *It wasn't me.*

It wasn't me.

It was our secret. Mine and Rosie's. Another one. She used that power in all sorts of ways. It became an instrument to bribe me with, 'If you don't do as I say, I'll tell them you killed the baby. Katherine already thinks it was you. I'd only need to say, and then you'd be punished for the rest of your life.'

It also became an instrument of intimacy. We cut our fingers, held them together, let the two bloods mingle. 'I'll never say a word.'

Olivia hated Rosie. I understood that. My loyalties were torn. She suspected me of loving her, but I didn't. I was afraid of her, even now. I depended on her silence. I was grateful.

Rosie came into the garden that night when we were out there. I'd only just got up. Olivia thought I was depressed, but I wasn't depressed. I was cornered. Wherever I looked, he was there. All the time. The child whose life I'd snuffed out. I had no right to depression. The best I could do was bear it, because it would never leave. Time overwhelmed me. Thoughts of the rest of my life began to give me vertigo.

Olivia and Rosie fell out. I'd never seen Olivia angry before – she was not given to public displays of unacceptable behaviour. She was, truly, a beautiful person, and she struggled to understand people who were unpleasant, who hurt others, because they were so at odds with who she was. It took a lot to rouse her and even that night, she just walked away, managing her anger. Rosie said I should leave her to calm down. She'd be OK. But I doubted it. I doubted whether anyone would ever be OK again. Misery fascinated Rosie. She had a calling as a voyeur. She liked to see it. She liked to touch it. Perhaps it was cathartic. She had the ancient Christian compulsion to walk in someone else's shoes and feel their pain. It was only afterwards that she liked to increase it for them.

She said, 'How's Katherine these days?'

I said, 'She puts on a brave face.'

People always asked after Katherine. They never asked after my father. He had not carried a cluster of cells in his body, or brought forth life in agony. Those were the only differences, but they made him less of a tragic figure. Always, Katherine would hold the monopoly on sadness and public sympathy.

'And how are you?'

The question was loaded with meaning, of course. We hadn't spoken about it since I'd left and gone to school.

'I'm living with it.'

'How?'

I thought, *You should have some idea.*

I shrugged.

She lit a cigarette and offered me one. I took it gratefully.

I said, 'The only way to live with guilt, as far as I can see, is to push it away and not think about it.'

'Or face it.'

I stared at her. She smirked, that old smirk I remembered from when we were children. I said, 'Impossible.'

She looked at me and said, 'Do you find it hard – pushing it away?'

'Sometimes. I was mad at school for a while, but I settled down. It helped that I never saw Katherine. Then Olivia…'

'You two are together?'

'Yes.' I always admitted it if people asked me. Olivia was more discreet.

'I thought so.' There was triumph in her tone.

'Having her with me helped. We lived in our own world at school. I didn't have to think about it too much. When you're far away, it's easier not to remember what went on, or what still goes on.'

'And now?'

'Now it's awful,' I said, simply.

Rosie inhaled deeply. She said, 'Katherine thinks it was me, you know.'

I didn't know. That was a shock. I said, 'Really? Are you sure?'

'Positive. Years ago, before you even went to school, she used to come round and rant at Alison. She thought it was both of us, but mostly, she thought it was me.'

I stayed silent.

Rosie went on, 'She didn't just tell Alison. She told anyone she could who would listen.'

'I know.'

She tipped her head back and blew out a set of smoke rings. 'It doesn't matter that much. The fact is, the whole village thought she'd gone bonkers. I used to laugh at it, the way they talked about her, when I always knew the truth.'

She was silent for a while, then carried on. 'I never cared. I still struggle to care. He was just a baby. His life had hardly even begun. There was barely anything there to kill.'

I'd been through this in my own head, many times. But it wasn't true.

She said, 'Do you care?'

I looked away from her.

'I take it that's a no.'

I stayed silent.

She said, 'What I do care about is that there's a question mark over me wherever I go. You know – 'Oh, there goes the girl that Katherine thinks killed her baby. I wonder if she really did.' – That's the trouble, isn't it?

They'll never be sure.'

I knew what she was building up to. *Tell them it was you, and only you.* I skirted around it. 'Most people have forgotten it by now. It was a long time ago.'

'They haven't forgotten. It still gets talked about.'

I nodded.

She edged closer towards me. The sky was growing darker, and I thought of Olivia inside the house, preparing to leave, and I wanted to go to her. I wanted to stop her, keep her here.

Rosie said, 'I want you to tell them.'

'What?'

'I want you to tell them I had nothing to do with his death. I want you to tell them you were the only one.'

'I…'

Her tone became sharp. 'I want you to tell them this, Leila. It's me who has to live here. You don't. You're going away again. All these years, I have taken the blame, but you were the one…'

'I was the one they sent away, Rosie. I was the one being punished.'

She laughed derisively. 'That wasn't punishment. Going away to a posh school, getting an expensive education …Believe me, Leila. That is not punishment where I come from. That's privilege.'

She stared at me, and I looked away. She was right, of course. By killing someone's child, I'd secured the future now stretched out before me, being constantly spun like gold.

Then she said, 'If you don't tell them, I've been thinking that perhaps I will.'

'Please don't.'

'I might. I'll start with Olivia. I'll tell her first.'

'Rosie…'

'And then I'll tell your father. And I'll tell them both that you have let me take the blame for all this time, and that you can sit there now, unrepentant as ever. You're not sorry. I can see you're not sorry.'

I looked at her. I said, 'I'll tell them.'

She sat back and handed me another cigarette. 'Good,' she said. 'That's good.' She reached out, and ran a cold hand down my cheek. 'I'm sure they'll forgive you, if you tell them. You were nine years old. They can't do anything to you. You were too young.'

'I know.'

My guilt was absolute. There was no way to absolve it.

Rosie said, 'They'll forgive you. Then you can forgive yourself, too, and move on.'

'I can't do that.'

'You can. Get me off the hook. Tell them it was you. Repent and get them to forgive you.'

It sounded simple. The thought of facing Katherine made me feel sick. Besides that, she already knew, and so did my father. My father might forgive me. She wouldn't.

In the end, it all came down to blood and water.

•

I didn't sleep that night. Rosie's words hovered on my mind, like flies on shit. I couldn't push them away. Actually, they were nuggets I held on to – I wanted faith in an absolution.

I lay awake next to Olivia, and indulged myself in fantasy. I would face them, they would forgive me, and they would end up back together. A healing balm. They'd stay here at Ash Farm, bringing up their three children with joy. I moulded the fantasy to the extreme. I saw myself in the future, visiting – the eldest child, once banished, now forgiven. I would bring bags full of surprises. The children would clamour to greet me. They'd treat me to sticky kisses. It would never cross their minds that I had once hurt one of their tribe. They would never know. I would treat these three as jewels. My precious jewels, our drops of gold.

The sun was coming up. It was five or six. I didn't know. September. I had no idea what time the sun rose. Perhaps that was a soul-deficiency in me – yet another sign that I was not at one with the world.

For another hour or two, I slept and woke. I couldn't tell the difference between thought and dream – they merged into one. I saw myself standing before Katherine. I'm very sorry. I must tell you I killed your child. Yes, you heard me correctly. Oh, I know you already know, but I thought admitting it could help. I don't expect you to forgive me, but it would be nice if you could. And while you're at it, why don't you get back together with my father? He loves you. I know it'll break his heart to leave the children and move out.

I had it planned, what I would say. *Sorry* struck me as being the key, the way in, the vital vocabulary for begging forgiveness. But even I could see that it fell pathetically short of what I meant. My verbal skills would limp and fail me. There needed to be a new language, I thought, for things that needed to stay sharp, and not be watered down by words. Narrative could only go so far. Pile sorry upon sorry, and I'd be in danger of overstatement. Redundant. Insincere.

Isaac started crying. I heard Katherine get up. It must have been seven, or thereabouts. These days, my father was sleeping in the spare room downstairs.

I was awake now, wired on adrenaline, and I could see no point in putting it off. I went through the usual rituals of showering and applying make-up and choosing what to wear. Small things. At times of great crisis or drama, you'd think the smaller things in life would be rendered irrelevant, but to me, they were crucial. You could get lost in the vastness of your own disastrous canvass. Small things were about all that rooted me in the world. I painted my nails pale pink, applied tiny jewels to my thumbs. I looked in the mirror. In what was probably some last-ditch attempt at innocence, I'd dressed in white. The ethereal eldest sister, the vulnerable adult child.

Olivia woke and sat up in bed. 'What are you doing?'

I turned round and said, 'I'm going to talk to Katherine and my father. I'm going to tell them it was me, not Rosie.' Even to me, my words carried a ring of the unreal.

She said, 'Are you sure?'

'Yes. Yes, I think so.'

'Why?'

That was the question, of course. For whose sake was I doing this? Katherine's, so she could know, at last, the truth of how her baby died? Lying awake last night, I'd developed noble plans of discussing with her the best way she thought I could pay for my crime. There had to be a way. There had to be a purge, a cleansing. There had to be some way to get this blood of my hands.

So it was for my own sake that I was doing this. I wanted to be welcomed home. I wanted to be adored. More than that, I wanted to be told I hadn't ruined everything.

I said, 'Because it's time they knew.'

She was sitting cross-legged on the bed, wearing only the t-shirt she slept in. The t-shirt was a subtle hint, I knew. There was no point in her lying naked anymore, now that I was no longer interested. But I was interested. I could go insane desiring her. I just had other things on my mind, and sex and guilt have always been inextricably tied up.

I kissed her lips. 'Wait for me,' I said.

'Are you doing it now?' she asked, disbelieving.

'Yes.'

'Are you really sure you want to?'

'No. Of course not. But don't try and talk me out of it.'

As I walked downstairs, I could feel myself stepping out of myself. I would face it like an actress. My great stage.

•

Downstairs, the kitchen hissed. Sunday morning. The Aga burned spilt fat. The room smelled of bacon and coffee. Lily, for the first time that day, was lying on the floor, screaming and kicking her legs. Katherine, tranquil and unperturbed as ever, was winding Isaac in the rocking chair.

She spoke to Lily from where she sat. I wanted to hear her shout, or lose her temper. She never had, that I'd seen. Only with me, after Alfie.

I said, 'Hi, Katherine.'

She turned and looked at me, nodded her acknowledgement, then focussed on the baby again.

She'd hardly spoken to me all summer. I couldn't blame her for that. We hung round the boundaries of politeness, but I knew she wanted to wallop me one. Beneath the calm and the care, she was seething. I'd made her life so unfair.

'Where's dad?' I asked.

'Out. I don't know where.'

I didn't know how to begin a conversation in the middle of Lily's tantrum. I wanted her to stop. I bent down in front of her. She didn't look up, and went on screaming.

'Leave her. She's fine.'

I wondered how she could say that. The child was insane. Temporarily, no doubt, but certainly insane.

She raised her head from the ground. Her face was bright red and soaked with tears. Her cries were beginning to sound hoarse. She choked on them. I handed her a plastic beaker of milk from the table. She hit it away and carried on. As always, Katherine was watching me. She said nothing.

I sat down on the floor.

Katherine said, 'She'll stop soon.'

I wondered how she did this – three children, twenty-four hours a day. There had to be a technique to it, something mysterious that was revealed when you gave birth. Because there was something saintly about motherhood. Selfless. I was sure they must all be raging underneath, longing to hurl a few chunks of abuse at someone, instead of that incessant love and tolerance.

I picked Lily up and held her in my lap. She kicked her legs. I grabbed hold of them and held them. The skin beneath my fingers turned red.

Panic-stricken, I let go and she stopped screaming, but she still cried. She reached up and put her arms around my neck. I was stunned, and oddly touched. I stood up, and carried her back to Katherine.

For once, Katherine laughed. She sat Isaac in his bouncer on the table and lifted Lily onto her lap.

She said, 'Do you want breakfast, Leila? There's bacon in the fridge. I think your father left some.' Her tone was the warmest I'd heard it, but it still came with an edge.

'It's all right. I only really drink tea first thing.'

'Is that something they teach you at boarding school?'

'What?'

'Not to eat.'

'No. It's instinct. We were all very good at it.' I heard the destructive note to my voice, and reined it in. I smiled. 'Would you like a cup of tea?'

'No, thank you.'

She was looking at me curiously. Ever since I arrived home, I'd avoided being in a room on my own with her. Filling the kettle with water, I could see that my hands were shaking. It surprised me, because although I felt cold inside, I was also quite calm and rational. Detached from what I was about to do, and its outcome, whatever that might be. I thought I was doing the right thing.

Lily was settled again. Katherine put her on the floor. She ran off to the playroom to join Grace. Convenient. I had no excuse now.

I let the tea brew.

I sat down at the table. Isaac chewed a felt book and smiled. He was two months now – three weeks older than his older brother.

Katherine picked up the bouncer. 'I'm going to get dressed,' she said. 'Will you be down here for a while? Could you make sure the girls don't attack each other?'

She started walking towards the stairs.

I said, 'Katherine, wait.'

She turned round.

'I'd like to talk to you.'

'About?'

I didn't like that tone. It carried a hint of derision, an undercurrent of, *And what could* you *possibly have to say that would interest* me*?* But I held on to the fact that, less than a minute ago, she was ready to trust me with her girls. That was an improvement. A start. A foundation to build on, albeit a flimsy one.

I said, 'Could you come here and sit down?'

She held out her arm and looked at her watch. 'I'm very busy, Leila.'

'It won't take long.' Wishful thinking on my part.

She came nearer, but didn't sit down. She put the baby and the bouncer on the worktop, and stood with her back against it.

I said, 'I was very sorry when my father told me you two were separating.'

'Yes. It's a pity. But that's life.'

The derision came to the surface. It was no longer an undertone, but I'd gone too far to step backwards. I said, 'I know this doesn't change anything for you, Katherine. I know how inadequate it is, but I want you to understand – to know – that I'm very, very sorry.'

She looked uncertain. 'Yes. You've just said that.'

I shook my head. 'No. I didn't mean…'

She was interested now, despite herself. The word, for all its limpness, had hooked her. She spoke slowly. 'What is it, then – exactly – that you're sorry for? Is this sympathy, or are you apologising for something? I'd like you to explain.'

I held her gaze. 'For Alfie.'

'For his death?'

'Yes.'

'You're sorry he died?

'No.'

She raised an eyebrow.

I said, 'Of course. Yes, of course I'm sorry he died, but that's not what I mean.'

'So what do you mean?'

She wasn't going to make this easier for me.

I said, 'I mean, I'm sorry –'

She sneered. 'You're sorry you killed him? Is that what you mean, Leila?'

Her voice was thick with fury. It hung from every syllable. It was terrifying. Under the table, my hands were trembling. My mind retreated. I looked away from her.

'Is that what you mean, Leila?' she demanded again.

'Yes,' I said. 'Yes. That's what I mean.' The calm of my voice was startling. An onlooker might call me remorseless.

She laughed. Bitter laughter, hard and vinegary. 'I wish, Leila, I really wish that your father were here to hear this.' She stopped speaking for a moment, turned her head and took deep breaths. 'Actually, on second thoughts,' she continued, facing me again, 'I don't wish that. I don't wish that at all. Because he would rescue you, and I do not wish for you to be rescued.'

I stayed silent and watched as she came towards me. I thought, *She is going to beat me.* Instinctively, I raised my hands to my face. She came closer, and yanked them away. She spoke venomously. Saliva flew. 'So you come here, to my house, eight years later, and you sit here in my kitchen, and you have the audacity to tell me that you're sorry. You're sorry you killed my child.'

She paused for a while, catching breath. When she spoke again, her tone had changed. It was level and icy. Businesslike. 'You're sorry you killed my child. Do I have this right?'

I nodded.

'And what were you hoping to achieve from your apology, young lady?'

I looked away again.

'What were you trying to achieve?' she asked. 'Forgiveness? A happy family?'

I found my voice. 'No. No, of course not.'

'That's a relief, then, because let me assure you – you will never have either of those things. You – *you* destroyed this family, Leila. You. Nobody else. Just you.'

I hung my head and stared at the grain in the table. Her words flew all around me.

'Do you have any idea,' she said, 'what it is like to lose a child you have given birth to?'

She stopped talking. She was waiting for me to answer.

'Would you like me to tell you?' she asked.

I had nothing to say. *Yes* and *No* would both be wrong.

'Would you like me to tell you?' she asked again.

'I –'

'The thing is,' she interrupted, 'the really bad thing is that I cannot tell you. I cannot tell you what it's like. Do you know why?'

Yes. Yes, I knew why.

'I can't tell you, because there are no words to describe something that horrific. That's why. That's why. But let me assure you, unless you ever lose your own child –and actually, I genuinely hope you never do – you will never even come close to understanding the enormity of what you did to me and to your father. Not to mention Alfie, whose life you took. His whole life. He was only five weeks old. Five weeks. Can you remember that?'

'Yes.'

'I always knew,' she said, triumphantly angry now. 'I always knew it was you, from the very first day. You and Rosie Ash.'

'It wasn't Rosie.'

She stared at me. Shock had made her silent.

'Rosie had nothing to do with it.'

'It was just you?'

I nodded.

'She did nothing?'

'Nothing.'

She laughed scathingly. 'Well, no wonder Alison told the entire village I'd lost my mind. No wonder.'

Isaac started crying. She went over and picked him up, and held him over her shoulder. With her back to me, she said, calmly, 'You're lucky I have three children, Leila. You're very lucky.'

She turned round again. 'Because if they didn't need me, I would risk the jail sentence, and I'd probably kill you.' She paused, rubbing her hand up and down Isaac's back. 'Actually, do you know what I have wished, every day, for the last eight and a half years?'

No, I don't know, I thought. *I can't imagine. Go on. Surprise me.*

'I have wished, every day, that you would die. Yes. Every single day, that is what I longed for. But not straight away. I wanted you to suffer first. But the fact is, Leila, you will never suffer enough. Nothing you go through can come close to what we have been through – and will continue to go through – because of you.'

This wasn't talk. She meant it. I could see that.

I said, 'I'm sorry. I should never have come…'

'You're right. You should never have come. But I have waited eight years for the chance to say this to you, and now I have. So thank you for giving me that.'

I sent her my words silently. *You're very welcome. It was my pleasure to hear it. I'm glad you got it off your chest. It doesn't hurt yet. But it will. It will. For the rest of my life, I am never going to get those words out of my head.*

I said, 'I'm very sorry.'

She didn't look at me. She grabbed the bouncer off the worktop and walked away towards the stairs. It was over.

It was over.

IV

Olivia

Her confession confounded me for days. I'd received the truth about her mysterious past straight from Leila. There was no enigma now. My girl was a murderess.

A murderess. It was more tolerable, as a piece of vocabulary, than murderer. But even so, no matter how I dressed it up in darkly feminine, Victorian-sounding language, the fact remained the same: she'd killed her baby half-brother.

Why had she not told me before? Perhaps I would never have fallen for her, if I'd known her first as a murderess. But I knew, really, that I would have done. Her past, when we were at Rotherfield, was far away and irrelevant. She would still have been Leila. In almost every way, she still was Leila; it was just that her past had caught up with us, and I was now faced with the bizarre reality of being in love with a murderess. (My mind reeled at the idea of what my mother would say. It was perhaps the only time I could imagine her saying, *But surely a murderer would suit you better than this, darling.*)

I thought, *She didn't tell me. She knew, all the time, what she had done, and she lived with it. I wondered whether she'd made light of it in her own head, though it seemed impossible to me. Maybe she just never thought about it. Or maybe she didn't care.*

I had to turn my back on those thoughts. Perhaps I'd re-visit them later, when years had passed and I was older and less naïve, and better able to face them. At the moment, if those things were true, then the girl I'd adored, almost since the day I first met her, was a fiction – nothing more than a beautiful trick of my imagination. I could never have been that wrong.

So.

I was never sure why people had to be defined by their life's major traumas. *Divorcee, widow, orphan.* I knew the events that created those titles were huge, but did they really need to be the final characterisation? No. Divorcees and widows could remarry, and orphans could be adopted. Surely a victim, a criminal, a murderess, could cease to be one, too, with the passing of enough time. I knew that my father would have reminded me, in his staunchly Tory fashion, of that old leopard-spots analogy, which had always struck me as redundant, because, quite simply, people were not leopards. People changed more deeply than at skin level. Life wasn't always just about shedding skin, or casting off exteriors. In fact, the persona was probably the most constant part. People changed at their centres, their cores. Life would throw a crisis at them, they'd sink under it, and then years or only months later, they'd re-emerge, unrecognisable.

I knew that was what had happened to her. She was no more a murderess than I was. She was changeable, and she had changed. My trick of the light, my girl of the mothernight.

•

I waited for her while she spoke to Katherine. I worried. I hoped. I hoped, more than anything, for a resolution. I wanted her forgiven. I wanted the family to be repaired. I wanted her happy. I didn't want her to go abroad, living like a wanderer, aimlessly paying for her crime because she could think of no other way to live with the guilt. I wanted her with me. I wanted her to step into the future that was waiting for her, and I wanted her life to be kind. I thought, *It will be kind, because she deserves it to be.* I believed in the levelling out of pain and happiness, the unstoppable turn of the wheel of fortune.

I heard her coming up the stairs. I sat on the bed, ready to greet her with sympathy and a smile. She came in, looking pale and stunned.

I said, 'How was it?'

She laughed. 'Not quite as I'd hoped, if I'm honest.'

'Was your father there?'

'No.'

She reported Katherine's fury.

I said, 'There is no excuse for that.'

'For what?'

'For being so harsh.'

'There is,' she said. 'There really is.' She paused and shook her head, disbelieving. 'I am so stupid. What was I thinking? That she'd forgive me? Because of course she wouldn't. For God's sake, I ruined her life. And for once, that's not an exaggerated expression. I really did.'

Her self-loathing was absolute.

I took her hand in mine. I said, 'You've done all you can do now. You need to leave this behind.'

'I don't think I can.'

'You can. You can leave here. You've barely been back in the last eight years. You can stay away now, for the rest of your life. You can move to Oxford and start again. And if she can't forgive you, you can forgive yourself.'

'I can't. I…'

'It's going to destroy you if you don't.'

She looked away, and said nothing.

•

In the afternoon, we made a visit to Alfie's grave. Leila had never been before. She hadn't even gone to the funeral. She took flowers and arranged them among the others already there. It was the smallest and most crowded memorial in the cemetery. We looked at the cards that had been left by Katherine and Gus, separately. They didn't remember their son together.

Always incomplete without you.

We walked back to Ash Farm slowly. The ferocious heat of the summer was wearing off now, though it was still warm. The forecasters were predicting a bitter winter, impossible to imagine, though I was looking forward to it. The cold would be refreshing, and I wanted to leave Ash Farm and Katherine and the children, and set up a life in which, though there were miles between us, Leila was always with me, no longer a secret. And I wanted her upright.

It didn't occur to me, after all this, that upright could be impossible.

•

I became afraid now to leave her alone, with only her father to shield her from Katherine's fury. I knew I could be no physical defence, but I was never going to abandon her now, not now I understood the reasons for all her distance and sadness.

I decided not to go to Manhattan. I phoned my mother. 'I'm sorry to mess you around. I won't be coming home like I said I would.' I didn't know why I still called it *home*, apart from the fact that I had nowhere else.

There was silence at the other end. I thought at first it was the pause that followed as my words crossed the Atlantic. It wasn't. It was my mother pursing her lips. I knew that was what she'd done as soon as she spoke. 'So when will I be seeing you, Olivia?'

'I don't know. Christmas, maybe.'

'I thought you were excited to come home.'

'I was.'

'Then why the change of heart?'

'I'm very busy.'

'You're eighteen years old, Olivia. You don't know what *busy* means.' I could see her stretched out on a chaise longue as she spoke, examining her manicure, unaware of any irony. 'Is something going on?'

'No.'

'Is it all right with this girl's parents if you stay on over there?'

'Yes. It's fine.'

She paused, then said, 'Olivia, I don't want to be nosy, but is there a boy involved anywhere in this decision?'

'No.'

'You wouldn't tell me, anyway.'

I could hear the offence in her tone. I wasn't sure how she thought I could share intimate details of my life with her, when she and my father had made the decision when I was seven years old to only see me once a year. I said, 'Probably not.'

'Ok. Well, let me know if you need anything, won't you? Your father can wire you any money you need.'

'I'm all right.'

'Have you got everything you need for school?'

'I've left school.'

'I mean university. They call it school here.'

'Not yet, but I will.'

'And how do you look? Are you scruffy?'

'I'm comfortable.'

'Do you need new clothes?'

'Probably a few.'

'Do they have decent stores near you?'

'I don't know. I expect so. I only need jeans.'

'You could be so pretty if you tried.'

'Mum…'

'OK. Listen, I'll get daddy to wire you some money. Buy whatever you want. I don't want you to struggle. There's no need.'

'Thanks.'

'I was looking forward to having you here.' There was genuine sadness in that line, and I couldn't understand it. I thought perhaps she and my father were growing apart. They'd been together twenty-five years. It would make sense. I found them hard enough for a week.

'I'll come back at Christmas.'

'Make sure you do.'

We said goodbye. She promised to send me two thousand pounds. I had no idea what to do with it.

•

While we'd been out at Alfie's grave, Gus had come home, and Katherine had told him. She told him what Leila had said to her, and what she had said to Leila, and now he was furious.

At night, we lay in bed together, listening to them argue. We knew Katherine was drunk. I'd never seen or heard her drunk before. I'd never even seen her drink. She was pregnant; she was breastfeeding. This night, she didn't care. She guzzled her way through nearly two bottles of wine. I wondered whether it was a throwback to her youth – she did it with the air of one who'd once done it often. There was a resoluteness to it, as though she'd just sat back and said, *Screw it. Tonight, I will get off my face.*

Leila was beside me, though far away again. I could not comfort her, or speak. She wasn't interested in words. She wasn't interested in sex. She wasn't interested in anything but her own thoughts, and I could only imagine what they were. Despite everything, there were times now when the fibres between us felt as flimsy as a cobweb's.

Katherine's voice came towards us from downstairs. She was shouting. Despite the drink, she was still lucid. 'I don't know why you're always so determined to see me as the villain, Gus. It was her. For fuck's sake, she's admitted it. It was her.'

His response came in muffled tones I couldn't hear. I wondered whether this was the way they'd carried on since losing Alfie. I suspected it might have been.

I looked at Leila. She was lying still, her eyes shut tight, her hands pressed firmly over her ears.

•

In the morning, after Gus had left for work, dropping Grace off at school on his way, Katherine came into my room. She carried a large white envelope in her hand, and looked pale and ill and old.

She sat on the edge of my bed. It seemed irrelevant now, whether they found out about us or not. Leila's sexuality was probably rendered insignificant by the fact that she'd murdered their son. Even so, I did feel slightly self-conscious, if only because I was naked beneath the covers. Because I could think of nothing else to do, I simply smiled and said, 'Hello.'

She smiled back, weakly. Leila didn't look up.

When Katherine spoke, her voice was soft and calm. She said, 'I want to apologise to you, Leila, for what I said yesterday. I can't say that it wasn't true, but I shouldn't have spoken in anger.'

Leila's eyes were wide open, but blank.

Katherine said, 'I don't want you to suffer now, no more than I'm sure you already have. But I would like you to read these, and then to treat them as confidential.' She put the envelope on the table beside the bed.

She said nothing else. She stood up and walked away.

Leila continued lying still. She didn't respond.

V

Leila

Footprints. Broken. Broken. I must mend them. I must put them back together and return them to his mother. Here. Have these. Look. I mended them. There's hardly a crack now. See? See? I will fix what I can.

Photos. They were dividing up the photos. Alfie, Grace, Lily, Isaac. One for you, one for me. They were dividing everything they owned. Tables, chairs, rugs, beds. Photos were what they fought over. Only one of Alfie dead. Arguing over who wouldn't be the one to take it.

Dear Alfie. It is now one year since you went. I miss you badly. It hurts more than it did on the first day. I didn't think, at the time, that that would be possible. I used to think pain must have limits.

Dear Alfie. Two years have passed now. It does not get any easier.

Dear Alfie. You have a sister. A genuine smile has returned to my face, but you are still missing, and I am still heartbroken.

Dear Alfie. You are four now. What do you look like? I study your photos, and try adding four years to your face, but it's so hard to know. Your eyes used to be blue, like all babies'. What colour are they now? Brown, like your daddy's, I think. If we meet again, I worry that I will not recognise you, and you will be hurt.

Dear Alfie. Another little boy who shares your birthday is starting school today, but you are not. I wonder what you would be good at, and what you would struggle with, and what sort of teacher you would have.

Dear Alfie. I had you for thirty-seven days. You have been gone now for two thousand and six days. I wish I knew where you were. They say you are safe with God. I never believed in Him before we lost you, but now I believe with all my heart. I cannot cope with the thought of never seeing you again.

Dear Alfie.

Dear Alfie.

The letters were relentless. They went on and on. Pages and pages. She'd written to him nearly every day since he died. Every birthday. Every milestone. Every new birth. They were all intimately recorded. *They ask how many children I have. I say 'three', but always I am thinking of you. Four. Four is the real number. I worry that you are looking down, and feeling denied. I am not denying you; it's just that not everyone deserves to know about you.*

Collected letters. Collected Letters of a Bereaved Mother. She could have sold them. They'd have looked good, in blank ink on ivory paper, bound between the covers of a book.

She gave them to me instead. *Understand what you did, Leila.* The final twist of the knife.

•

I put the letters down, settled on the decision that had been swinging backwards and forwards in my mind for the last few months, and went outside. My father was sitting in the clearing among the fir trees, my place to hide when I was a child. I made myself safe there, though in reality, I was never in any danger. But small spaces were a comfort. It wasn't so enclosed now. Ever since hacking down the two other trees, it had become part of the garden. Of course, it wasn't a memorial. They couldn't face that, after finding my gift beneath the earth. They spent extra money on his headstone, and planted a tree in the park instead. A cruel reminder of growth.

He was smoking. I'd never seen him with cigarettes before. I sat on the grass beside him. 'I didn't know you smoked.'

'I don't. It's just this once.'

His forehead was beaded with sweat. 'I need to move some stuff this afternoon. Would you mind helping me?'

'OK.'

'I've been clearing out the cellar. Your mother's things are down there. Take whatever you want from the boxes.'

'I already have.' I showed him her ring that I wore around my neck. 'I took this when I was eight.'

'Well,' he inhaled on his cigarette. 'I suppose it's not the worst thing you ever did.'

'Dad…'

He said, 'Are you looking forward to starting at Oxford?'

I wasn't. I wasn't looking forward to it because I wouldn't be going.

I said, 'Yes.'

'You will always have a home to come back to now.'

'Thank you.'

Was this parental love? Love that would continue, foolishly, hopefully, even after – anyone could see – all hope for repair had gone? We could never get beyond this.

He looked at me. 'The school I sent you to. Was it OK?'

'It was fine.'

'You were happy?' His intonation merely hinted that this was a question. It was largely a statement, with a tiny crust of doubt.

'I was happy enough.'

'That's good. You had friends?'

'A few.'

'Olivia is very nice.'

'Yes.'

'The school wrote and told us about you two. Before you came home.'

'What do you mean?'

'You and Olivia. They were worried. They thought you needed separating.'

'Really?'

He smiled. 'But actually, I'm very glad you have her.'

I could tell from his tone that he knew. I didn't look at him. It wasn't a subject to approach with anyone's father.

I said, 'How often will you have the children?'

He sighed. 'Weekends.'

'I'm sorry.'

'It's not your fault.'

'I didn't mean that. I meant I'm sorry for you and Katherine. I'm sorry for the children.'

'They'll survive it. We'll make sure they're OK.'

I took a cigarette and smoked it silently.

He said, 'You can still come home, even when I've got them. Katherine has agreed to that. She knows you won't…'

A relief. A concession. Recognition on her part that it was a one-off. I was not a serial committer of infanticide. Small comfort. *Dear Alfie, I hope she bears the burden of this for the rest of her life.*

I said, 'What are you going to do with what's left of my mother's stuff?' Being unable to remember her made her a stranger. She had never been *mum*. She was distant. She would only ever be My Mother.

'I don't know. Do you want it?'

'Don't you?'

He said, 'That was another life.'

I paused. It wasn't something we'd ever discussed before. I had no idea who she was, or who he was before Katherine. I said, 'Was it happy?'

'What?'

'That life?'

'Yes.'

'Good.' I felt genuine relief.

'It was extremely happy, for a few years. You probably don't remember.'

'No.'

'Can you remember anything of that time before she died?'

'No.'

'You were very young. But we were all very happy. For five years.'

I'd done better than these three, then. I'd experience what they could never have. Perfect family happiness. A gift that could never last.

I wondered, *Who will put this right? Who will clear up the mess of all this blood?* I couldn't, but they might. What were their chances? It would only take one. Just one to grow up sane and undamaged. Or, if they had to be damaged, it would take just one to be dynamic enough to transform it into good experience. If that was possible.

I thought, *To my brother and sisters, I leave only my prayer that you will be OK.* Though what good my prayers would be were anyone's guess.

Dear Alfie. I pray every day that you are being cared for wherever you are. You must be somewhere. I cannot accept that I gave you life only to have it brutally snatched away. It is not possible. You must exist somewhere. I have never been jealous before, but I am jealous now. I am jealous of everyone who can see you.

I stubbed my cigarette out. My father looked at it and said, 'How long have you been doing that for?'

'About three years.'

'You should give up.'

'So should you.'

I said, 'You haven't told me where your new house is.'

'It's in the village. I want to stay here, for the kids.'

I thought, *They should stay together. He doesn't want to lose them, and she doesn't want to bring them up alone. If it can't be cleared, there should at least be a way to step over this mess.*

I said, 'Is this really the only way?'

'I can't think of any other. Believe me, I've tried.'

My newest crime. Inadvertent, but no less real for that.

'Does it,' I cleared my throat, 'does it really all go back to Alfie?'

He nodded. Then he said, 'But don't take that on. If we were different people, if you had been hers, who knows what might have happened?

'Well...'

'Why did you do it?' he asked.

'Sorry?'

'Why did you do it?'

'I don't know.'

'Try.'

I shook my head. I couldn't tell him. There was no point, and it would hurt him. I said, 'Do we have to go through this now?'

He sighed heavily. 'I suppose not.' He lit another cigarette. 'I want to ask you something, and I hope you'll answer truthfully.'

'OK.'

'Was there anything I could have done, after your mother died, that would have stopped you? That would have made you happy?'

I shook my head. 'No.'

'Are you sure?'

'Yes.'

'OK.' He seemed satisfied. He drew on his cigarette again. 'I'm sorry I sent you away.'

'It's OK.'

'I didn't want to.'

'It's fine.'

'There was desperation in my decision. I wanted to shield you from Katherine, and I couldn't leave her.'

'I know.'

'And I didn't want it getting public. For your sake. She'd have made it public. I thought it would make everything worse.'

'It would have done.'

'You've done well, though.'

'I've done OK.'

'I'm very proud of you.'

•

After that, I went next door to see Rosie. I'd managed to avoid her mother all summer, but now, in her own house, I had to speak.

She said, 'How have you found it, Leila, being back home?'

'Fine, thank you.'

'Rosie tells me you're going to Oxford.'

'Yes.'

'I didn't know you were that clever.'

I laughed politely. It was a standard line.

She carried on, 'I haven't seen Katherine for a while, but I suppose she must be busy with the new baby.'

'Yes.'

'How is he?'

'Great. He's smiling.'

'She must be so pleased.'

I said, 'Yes. She's very pleased to have a boy.'

She's so glad I haven't killed this one.

Rosie and I made our escape and went upstairs. In her room, Rosie said, 'Did you tell them?'

'Yes. I told Katherine it was me. I told her you had nothing to do with it.'

'Has she forgiven you?'

'Of course not.'

'So what happens now?'

'They split up, and life goes on.'

'That's it?' She looked disappointed.

'Yes. That's it.'

'When are you leaving?'

'The day after tomorrow.'

'Will you ever come back?'

'No.'

'Never?'

'Never.'

I left her house. I walked four miles to the next village. It was bigger than this one. It had a florist. I bought a bunch of white lilies for Olivia, and a single white rose for Alfie's grave. Peace.

VI

Olivia

Late in the evening, I watched her from my window as she came home. The sky unrolled behind her, flared red by the setting sun. She was walking eastwards away from it, back to the house and to me, and in the days and months and years that followed, I often remembered that scene: Leila, dressed in white, walking solitary, her arms laden with flowers, the sky her spectacular backcloth.

In two days, she'd be leaving for Oxford and I'd be going to Scotland. The miles between us were going to be long, but I wasn't afraid of them. In fact, I welcomed them. I knew now that we would never be truly apart. Her life had become mine, and all of mine was hers, and we could never have lived separately even if we'd wanted to. Life had locked us, each one inside the other, as solidly as if we'd traded flesh or blood.

I drew the curtains and lit the three ivory church candles Katherine had bought last week for the fireplace in my room. She and Gus and the children were away, and even though we had the whole house to ourselves, there was only one place we wanted to be, and that was here, in our room, in our world shut off from the world.

Leila opened the door and stepped inside. The flowers in her arms were pure white lilies, pungent and exquisite. 'I bought you these,' she said, and as she gave them to me, she kissed me, lightly but lingeringly on the lips.

I smiled. 'Thank you.'

I reached out and brushed my fingertips through her hair. It was full of tiny purple flowers that had wafted away from the bushes or the trees wherever she'd been sitting before she decided to come home. Some had fallen over her shoulders, and others clung to the white chiffon of her skirt. Even now, she could still make my stomach hurt when I looked at her.

'Where did you go?' I asked.

'Alfie's grave.'

I nodded as I unfolded the lilies from their layers of wrapping. Their scent was rich. It filled the room. An old china jug stood in a bowl on the mantelpiece. Leila picked it up and went to the bathroom to fill it with water. I arranged the lilies one by one inside it. Yellow pollen from their centres stained my fingers.

She sat down on the edge of the bed. The candlelight threw shadows against her face. She said, 'I finished reading Katherine's letters.'

'How were they?' I asked.

She shook her head. 'Awful,' she said. 'Absolutely awful.'

I sat down next to her. A late bee, drowsy and fat, attracted by the light and the scent, flew in through the window and hovered among the lilies.

Leila reached down and pulled some sheets of paper from the waistband of her skirt where she'd tucked them. She opened one out and her eyes skimmed over the page. 'She believes she'll see him again.'

'She has to.'

'I suppose so.' She paused, unfolding another letter. 'She believes in eternal love.'

She passed it to me, pointing out the neat, handwritten lines with her finger.

'There.'

I read. The date at the top was six years after his death. Now you have another sister. Soon, I will start telling her about you, so she knows who you are. I don't talk about you much anymore, but that doesn't mean I don't think about you all the time. You will never be gone. Until the day my life is over and we are reunited, you will live in my heart and in my mind, and that is where I keep you, safe from anymore harm. I cannot see you, but you are with me always. Love is, and always will be, stronger than death.

I passed it back to her.

'What do you think?' she asked

'What is there to think? I think it's tragic.'

'But I like the part about not being separated. Not even in death.'

'It's a nice idea.'

I was hesitant, unsure where she wanted this conversation to go. Did she want me to say, according to Katherine's philosophy, that it didn't matter that she'd killed Alfie? Because I couldn't say that. Eternal love might reign supreme, but it was always better if they could live. It gave me little comfort. I thought it would be easier, surely, if feeling dissolved in their last breath, and freed you when left behind. I could see that that was hopeless. I understood already what it meant to be rendered powerless by love that refused to die.

She folded the letters over and put them down on the bedside table. She sat beside me again and said, 'Do you like the flowers?'

'Yes.'

She kissed me, and traced her fingertips down my cheek. 'I'm sorry this hasn't been the summer you were dreaming of.'

'Don't worry about it.'

She leaned forwards and kissed me again, hard on the mouth. I responded. It felt as though years had passed since we'd been together like this.

She moved closer and pushed me back on the bed. Her breathing came fast and heavy as she fought with my clothes. She murmured that she loved me, then she wound her legs around my waist and trapped me underneath her. I gasped. I wrapped my arms around her neck and pressed my lips and my tongue on hers again. She yanked her skirt up to her waist. Beneath it, she was naked. I hadn't seen her or touched her for so long, for a second I just gazed at her. I grabbed her and pulled her back down against me, moving my legs wide apart, then closing them tight around her. She closed her eyes. Her breathing turned to noise. I raised my hips from the bed, pushing against her as hard as I could, and we moved and moved and moved together, until suddenly she slowed down and said, 'Come with me,' and I did.

Afterwards, she lay naked and breathless beside me. It was dark outside. The candles beside us gleamed and flicked. She rolled over onto her front and draped her arm across my chest. I took her hand and held it in mine, and I tried to imagine that this was the hand that had stifled the breath from a baby. I couldn't. These were new hands now. Time had washed them white as lace. She was no more a murderer than I was.

We slept. I didn't hear her leave, but I woke at daybreak and she was gone. On the table beside the bed, she'd left a tiny purse, about one inch square, made from pale pink beads. I opened it. Inside was an ivory heart, made of shell or mother-of-pearl, and a note on pink paper.

Eternally, Leila.

•

I went back to sleep, then re-awoke around nine. Next to me, her side of the bed was still empty. She was often doing this recently – wandering off without mention of where she was going. I put on my dressing gown and walked along the hall to her room. She wasn't there.

I called, 'Leila!'

She didn't answer.

I called again.

Silence. The scent of lilies drifted onto the landing.

I went downstairs and made myself breakfast and read a magazine of Katherine's. She was starting work next week, as a supply teacher, and she'd employed a part-time nanny for Lily and Isaac. I'd heard her arguing about it with Gus. She didn't want to leave the children – he said she wouldn't have to if he stayed – she said she'd never again live in a house where Leila could visit. That was the end of it. They were never going to move beyond Leila.

At ten o'clock she still wasn't home, so I went upstairs and packed the last of my things. Considering the wealth of my parents, I didn't own very much. Most of my belongings were in their apartment in Manhattan, but as I hardly ever went back there, they were of little use to me. My mother told me last week that they were depositing the two thousand pounds into my bank account as soon as they could, so I could buy everything I needed for the new term. This was in addition to my monthly allowance for food and books and a social life (something else I was looking forward to re-claiming, once we'd left here). I didn't know what she thought I'd need, but more than anything, I found that I was craving furniture. I wanted an antique desk and a chaise longue. I wanted curtains that draped to the floor. I wanted to own things that would root me in the world. A life without possessions was too easy to dismantle, pack up, take somewhere new.

I heard footsteps on the path outside and look up out of the window. It was Katherine coming home, with Isaac curled up in his sling against her chest, and Lily dangling from one hand. They'd been to her parents' house for the night. I had no idea where Gus had been. I'd thought he was with them, though of course he wouldn't be, not anymore.

I got dressed, slipped the heart Leila had left me into my pocket, and wandered back downstairs. Katherine smiled at me as I walked into the kitchen. 'Is Leila in?' she asked.

I shook my head. 'I don't know where she is. She left early. She was out when I woke up.'

'Right. It's just that Gus needs her to help him move some things to his new place. Could you remind her when you see her?'

'OK.' Then again I said, 'I don't know where she is.'

She looked unconcerned. 'She'll be back.'

She unhooked Isaac from his sling and laid him down in the carrycot in the corner. Lily was industriously carrying sets of pirates and farm animals from the floor and dumping them in a wooden trolley already loaded with wooden bricks and tubs of play dough.

I said, 'Do you need any help with anything?'

'No. It's fine. Thank you.'

I took my jacket from where it hung by the kitchen door. 'I'm going out for a while. I'll be back soon.'

I wanted to find Leila. She'd been gone too long.

Out on the lane, my first thought was that she'd be back at the churchyard, arranging flowers on the graves, easing death with beauty. I walked straight there. I stood at the entrance and looked, shielding my eyes from the sun. I couldn't see her. Instinctively, I stepped through the gate and went over to the two graves: Alfie's and her mother's. They were close together.

What I found was a card she'd left by Alfie's headstone, tied around a single white rose. There were no words, only the date, which was today's, and her initial: *L.*

I read it, and put it back.

I left the churchyard and began to walk around the village, up the main street, past the post office and the school, and then out onto the other side of the lane where she lived. I told myself not to worry. She was nowhere, but it was morning, and broad daylight. I didn't need to panic, or start imagining a parallel life where I'd lost her. I put my hand in the back pocket of my jeans and took out the purse and the heart. Eternally, Leila.

Fear piped through me like water. It trickled; then rushed.

I broke into a run back to Ash Farm. Katherine was in the living room, breastfeeding Isaac while Lily watched children's television. I kept my tone light and asked, 'Has Leila appeared yet?'

'No. I haven't seen her. But don't worry. She'll be back.'

I looked at her and thought, *But you don't care. You don't care at all what happens to her.*

Gus still wasn't back. I went out again by myself, hunting the woods and the orchard. I searched for her in the clearings among the trees, and on beds of damp earth. Time went by. Now and then, lost among the larches, I called her, and now and then, I thought I heard her reply. I waited, and listened.

She stayed faint and elusive as angels.

•

Hours passed. Morning drifted to afternoon; afternoon became evening; and then the sun set and the darkness fell, and still she did not come home.

Even Katherine began to look worried. At ten, Gus called the police. Then he called the hospitals, and as I listened to him speak, Leila was suddenly no longer mine, but his. She wasn't my lover. She was his child, only seventeen years old, female and vulnerable.

A policeman came round to the house. He listened to us. We told him what we knew. He asked if Leila had any reason to run away. We said no.

He went away again. Gus took a torch and went outside to try and find her. From the kitchen, we heard his car start.

Katherine said, 'Try not to worry too much.'

I nodded. Fear blocked my throat. Occasionally, for a few seconds, I felt as though I wasn't quite there. I was outside my body, looking in, watching from somewhere far away, and I was numb, because from that awful, far-off place, *I knew.* I knew, and I knew, and I knew.

For a long time, neither of us spoke. Nervously, Katherine fingered the gold chain around her neck, then eventually she said, 'This is awful. I hope he finds her. I hope she's OK.'

I stared at her. I remembered the letters to Alfie. I have lost my capacity to be reasonable, or humane, or objective. I am so, so angry. I want her never to experience joy. I want her to know only sorrow and guilt. And if I'm honest, what I really want is to see her dead.

I said, 'I hope so, too.'

She struggled to find words. 'I know how important she is to you.'

I thought, *No, you don't. You have no idea.*

She drew a deep breath. 'I'm sure that if...After Alfie...Perhaps...'

She shook her head and gave up.

I knew what she was trying to say. If it weren't for the fact that she killed my child, I might be able to like her.

I thought about Rosie. Gus had phoned her earlier. Like everyone else, she hadn't seen Leila since yesterday. I wondered if that were true. I thought, *Perhaps they are together now...*

The hands on the clock kept moving, too fast. The more time that passed, the more I thought, *She isn't coming home.* I tried to imagine a future without her, and couldn't. It looked long and bleak. And empty.

Gus's car pulled back into the drive. He came in, looking drawn and white. 'I can't find her.'

I looked at the door, and thought, *Now come home.*

I continued looking. I stared and stared, but it didn't matter how hard I stared, she still would not walk in.

He said, 'If she's missing, we simply need to look for her. I will cover every inch of ground until I find her. The world is not that big.'

It made sense, in a way, though even I, in my anxious state, could see that hunting the earth, on the lookout for someone who wasn't static, was a tough call. I wondered if there were enough years in his life left to do that. Then I wondered what we would do, if we never found her.

•

The next morning, she was still gone. The police returned, taking it seriously. They told us they would go to the press if she hadn't been found by evening. One of them said, 'We need to begin the hunt here. We'd like to search the house.'

Gus said, 'I've already done that.'

'Nevertheless, we'd still like to look.'

He stood back and let them.

No one had slept. Katherine took Grace to school and Lily to her mother's. When she came back, Gus was upstairs to talk to the policemen again. I heard them searching bedrooms, and the sound of furniture being moved across the floor. They were leaving no inch of space untouched.

Doors opened and slammed shut. Katherine said, 'It will kill him to lose her.'

I said, 'I know.'

Suddenly, from upstairs, we heard him bellow.

Katherine looked at me. I felt cold and shaky. My stomach lurched and I gagged, though I wasn't sick.

I thought, *I cannot move. I cannot know what he knows.*

Katherine took my hand and gripped it. One of the policemen came into the room, grave-faced and solemn. For a moment, he hung his head, then he said, 'I'm very, very sorry. I'm afraid we've found her.'

•

She was dead. Leila was dead.

They covered her in a sheet and carried her away. Then days went by, and nights went by, and I didn't know how many. I tried to count them. But time and numbers dissolved into nothing. I heard Katherine on the phone. She was saying, 'It happened three days ago,' but I couldn't split the world into days anymore. There was only space. Sometimes it was dark, and sometimes it was light, but Leila was always gone and there was nothing else.

•

We knew it was suicide, but they needed a post-mortem anyway. I wanted to speak to the pathologist. I wanted to tell him: Please be careful. She doesn't like to be touched by strangers. I didn't want him studying her, or cutting into her. I didn't want him taking her heart in his hands and examining it. It was hers. It was intimate. It wasn't meant to be seen, or held.

•

I stayed in bed, and didn't move. Rosie brought me flowers. She arranged them in a vase and left them on the mantelpiece, by the lilies that were old and wilting. I wanted them to disappear. They tired me. They were red, and vibrant, and demanded my energy. I was supposed to admire their beauty, their scent, keep them alive. But I didn't want the responsibility of flowers. I didn't care whether they lived or died.

•

Sometimes, I woke, and I prayed for her to come back. I reached into the space beside me, feeling for her. She wasn't there, and she wasn't there. I closed my eyes. I smelled the flowers. I wept.

•

Katherine abandoned her job and stayed beside Gus. I heard them talking. I heard them arguing. I went downstairs and saw them embracing. Later, I heard him say, 'You've got what you wanted,' and her say, 'No.'

•

She phoned my parents. She said, 'They were very close.' My mother came over on the first flight to England. We left Ash Farm and stayed in a hotel, waiting for the funeral. I didn't speak. It took all my energy just to lie down on the bed and stay alive. She made a doctor come out and visit me. He prescribed anti-depressants or tranquillisers, I wasn't sure which. I was aware of them speaking. He said, 'She's had a terrible shock. Her body needs to catch up with her.'

I gazed upwards at the ceiling. *Her body needs to catch up with her.* A strange expression, I thought, as though my soul had already departed.

•

The church was thick with the smell of flowers and sweat. The organ churned its bleak refrains. People kept coming and coming, suited, dressed in black. I sat in silence. I could hear the formal tap of shoes against the brick floor, the sombre murmuring of voices, the whispered shock: She is dead.

We held the front pew – me, Gus and Katherine. Rosie was somewhere, too, lost among faces. The vicar in his robe shuffled papers, preparing his speech. I thought, *What can he have to say about Leila that can be true?* He didn't know her.

I was dressed in white. A long white dress with a tiny red rose at the hem. I embroidered it there myself two days ago. No one here knew that I wasn't just her friend. No one knew. No one knew how pure this grief was. Except me. And her.

The notes of the organ altered. People stood and fell silent. Katherine touched my shoulder with her hand. I thought, *I will not bear this. I will not last.*

I didn't turn around. I looked forwards. I looked at the flowers – so many of them – and thought, They cannot fool me with their life and their scent and all their beauty. What balm is there for this?

They carried her closer. They crossed the threshold into my vision, and then came nearer. The coffin was laden with roses. I closed my eyes. *My God, Leila, you are so cruel.*

I watched as they set the coffin down, five feet away from me. I focussed my gaze on the lid. I thought, *Don't fob me off with all your pretty notions of eternal love. You are dead and I am here, and you have trapped me, because I cannot stop loving you. There is nothing blessed about this. This is not romantic. You are dead, and I am here.*

We sat down. The vicar spoke. I didn't listen, or hear. The post-mortem had put her death late in the morning of September 23rd. The police found her body in the attic, the old bedroom she used to sleep in as a child. There was alcohol in her blood, and empty bottles on the floor where she died. So she'd still been alive while I was searching for her. She was up there, in the attic, drinking herself to courage, while I called her name.

One of our old teachers from Rotherfield Hall gave a speech. *Full of promise*, she said about Leila. *So conscientious and clever.* I thought, *But she was so much more than that. You have no idea.*

She stopped talking and sat down. The organ started again. We sang hymns. All the while, the coffin stood at the front of the church, and I knew she was lying inside it, but I found it impossible to grasp. They hadn't let me see her before, when they'd kept her in the mortuary, cold and scarred. I was still expecting her home. I was furious with her, and I wanted her to know. I thought, *You knew what this would do to me, and yet still you did it. I would never have done this to you. You were enough to keep me alive.*

The hymns and the speeches stopped. They lifted the coffin, and we followed it slowly outside. The sun shone over the churchyard. The ground was still hard from the summer's lack of rain. I walked beside Katherine, her arm draped loosely around my shoulders. I was easier to support than Gus. He was still stunned, and silent.

There were only the three of us at the burial. The piece they'd put in the local paper read, *For family members only* and despite everything, I was touched to be thought of as family. The others had all returned to Ash Farm now. Katherine's mother was there with the girls and the baby, and my mother was there as well, preparing food for the wake.

We stood together beside the grave. The vicar prayed. His words passed over me. They began lowering her into the ground. I watched, and felt my life close. Sorrow took its place in my body, making itself permanent.

We each had one flower to throw onto the coffin. I threw mine. A single red rose. It was wet and heavy, and made a dull thump on the wood as it landed.

Part Four

Autumn

Two weeks after the funeral, Gus had moved out. He lived now in a two-bedroom cottage on the other side of the village, renting it until he summoned the strength to find somewhere to buy. He said he wouldn't be buying a big house again. There was no point. He was scaling down, minimising, making do – as far as Katherine could see – with nothing but the bare essentials: a room for himself, and a room for the children to share when they stayed.

She felt guilty for still living at Ash Farm. By rights, it should be his – he'd paid for it; he'd owned it for years before she came along. On Friday evening, when she dropped off Grace and Lily, she'd suggested that they sell it and halve the money, but he refused. 'It's their home,' he said. 'Let them keep it.'

She worried about him, and she worried about the girls staying with him. It was Sunday, and they were there now, and she wasn't convinced he was in any fit state to look after them alone for a whole weekend so soon.

But they were all he had. She couldn't deprive him of these children, too.

What she wanted, perhaps unrealistically, was for him to come home. They might never rekindle what they'd lost over the years. They might never be living together, blissful and carefree as she'd once planned, but they shared too much now. She knew that neither of them would meet anyone else after all this. The chaos had grown too huge, and no one else could ever understand. They could either march relentlessly onwards to the end – making the best of what was left, staying alive for the sake of the children – or they could re-unite, and at least share their tragedy between them. Even if it was just from compassion and desperation, she did still love him.

He wouldn't do it, of course. He'd never said so, but she knew he blamed her. He blamed her for being so resolutely unforgiving. He blamed her for her honesty when Leila confessed. He blamed her for making Leila read her letters to Alfie, for forcing her to realise the enormity of her crime, when the truth was that she already knew it, and was simply managing her life in the best way she could.

Leila's note to her father when she died simply read, *Sorry*. She said nothing to Katherine, and as far as Katherine knew, nothing to Olivia.

Olivia. Katherine's heart went out to her. She'd left with her mother after the funeral, stricken and ill. Katherine had wondered what she'd do. She'd been due to start university the day after Leila's death, but before the funeral, when Katherine asked if she still planned to go, she'd shaken her head. She wasn't strong enough for the change, her mind was overwhelmed with thinking about Leila – she couldn't focus on studying, and certainly wasn't lively enough to attract friends, or to party her way through the first term like they would.

But she wrote. She wrote last week to say that, actually, she had gone. She was living in a hall overlooking the sea, and she'd met a few people, and she was OK. That was the word she used: OK. Katherine suspected it was a civilised exaggeration, that if Olivia had been honest, she was about as far from being OK as Gus was. But she would survive, Katherine was sure of that. Healing would take time, and might never be complete, but she had youth on her side, and youth counted for a lot.

She heard Gus's car pull up outside, in the driveway that split Ash Farm from the oast house next door, where Alison and Rosie lived. Two weeks ago, a *For Sale* board had gone up outside. 'For Rosie's sake,' Alison said. 'There are too many memories here.' Katherine envied that. She envied a troublesome past that could be abandoned with its location. Hers and Gus's could never be left so easily. The past was all they were made of.

He rapped on the side door. She stood up and opened it. 'You don't have to knock,' she told him.

He shrugged. 'I thought I'd better.'

Grace and Lily ran inside. Grace spilled out the news of her weekend – they'd been swimming, they'd made a miniature garden in a pot and put a mirror in as a pond. 'Look!' she insisted.

Katherine looked obediently, then the girls disappeared to the play room.

'Would you like to come in?' she asked.

He stepped over the threshold. They went to the kitchen and he sat down in the chair he always used.

She turned the kettle on. He watched her for a moment, then smiled and said, 'Do you have anything stronger?'

She opened the fridge and brought out a half-filled bottle of white wine. She poured two glasses and sat opposite him. 'Have they been OK?'

'They've been fine.'

'And what about you? How've you been?'

He shook his head. 'Not great. You?'

'Better than you, I expect, although…'

He looked at her.

'I'm sorry,' she said. 'I'm sure you blame me.' The words had left her mouth without her thinking about them. Instantly, she regretted them.

'I don't,' he said.

'Pardon?'

'I don't blame you. I don't blame anyone. There isn't anyone to blame, and looking for someone won't help any of us. We just have to live with what happened as well as we can.'

'Right. How's the cottage?'

'Small. Quiet tonight, I expect, when I go back there. I'll miss them.'

She cleared her throat and didn't look at him as she spoke. 'You don't have to go back if you can't face it. You can stay here.'

He said nothing.

Upstairs, Isaac began to cry. Katherine stood up. Gus stopped her, 'I'll get him,' he said. She sat back down.

The girls came back into the kitchen. 'Where's daddy?' Grace asked.

'Where's daddy?' Lily repeated, her baby voice lisping over the s.

'Upstairs with the baby. He'll be down soon.'

'Is he coming home?'

'I don't know.'

They disappeared again.

Gus came back down the stairs. Katherine took the baby from him, unbuttoned her top, and latched him on to her breast. His crying stopped.

Gus watched her. He said, 'How are you finding this? The three of them on your own?'

'It's not easy. It helps that I go to work, although I don't feel good about leaving them.'

When Leila died, she'd turned down the supply work she'd been offered at the school in the next village. It would have been for the whole term. Now, she was working in town, covering an infant teacher on sick leave. The agency promised her that more would follow, but she was homesick. She was homesick for her old life, even with the sadness that shadowed it. Pile tragedy on tragedy, she thought, and that was what happened.

Gus stood up. 'Where are the girls?' he asked. 'I'd better say goodbye.'

'You're going?'

'I think so.'

'You don't have to.'

He looked at her hesitantly. 'I…'

She reached out her hand, and laid it over his.

'Stay,' she said.

Acknowledgements

Love and thanks to my family:
My mum, Chris Barefield, and step-dad Keith Pitchford
My dad, Alan Stovell, and step-mum Penny Stovell

Thanks to:
Claudia Cruttwell, Susanna Griffiths, Karen Lockney

Also to:
The department of Creative Writing at Lancaster University
The Arvon Foundation

Extra thanks to:
Emma Barnes
and
Will Francis

Special thanks to:
Lisa Glass
Rosy Barnes
Maureen Lenehan
The wonderful folk at MsB

Love to:
Clay